Summer
Dance

MAEVE HENRY

A
Summer
Dance

MAMMOTH

First published in Great Britain 1994
by William Heinemann Ltd
Published 1995 by Mammoth
an imprint of Reed International Books Ltd
Michelin House, 81 Fulham Road, London SW3 6RB
and Auckland, Melbourne, Singapore and Toronto

Reprinted 1995

ISBN 0 7497 2377 7

A CIP catalogue record for this title
is available from the British Library

Printed and bound in Great Britain
by Cox & Wyman Ltd, Reading, Berkshire

For Emily

Chapter One

Helen could tell her sister had decided not to like the house even before they got out of the car. During the drive across town, Teresa had slumped in the back seat, sighing morosely if either of the other two tried to speak. She was a short, plump, pretty girl of fourteen, with chestnut hair and a high colouring unflattered by the convent uniform colours of maroon and sky-blue. Helen, thin and wiry, with pale skin and frizzy dark hair, sat forward alertly beside her, looking like a boy in the blue cords and white shirt of the comprehensive. She had failed the exam for the convent, not that she cared.

'Almost there now,' their mother said, glancing back at them in the mirror. Nicola Flynn was in her early forties, a taller, fairer version of Teresa. After a minute she added, 'We'll only be a few minutes from the beach.'

'And the town centre,' said Helen loyally.

But Teresa only stared, eloquently, out of the window.

They had taken the long way round, past the park and the church, and then along the coast road, before turning into the streets and streets of terraced houses that ran in crooked rows back to the railway line.

'Here we are, then.'

Their mother pulled in to park, and released her seat belt, but no one made a move to get out of the car.

'I still don't see why we have to move here,' Teresa said hollowly. 'I mean, look at it.'

'Don't be such a snob, Tess,' her mother replied crisply.

But even Helen found it difficult to say anything positive about the street they had parked in, and it looked worse when they got out and were all standing on the pavement. The afternoon sunshine showed up every shabby detail of the narrow houses; there wasn't even a dandelion to break up the monotony of the brick.

'I suppose ours is that one over there with the broken gate,' Teresa said, pointing across the road at a house distinguished from the others by its lack of a number and its peeling green paint. Helen watched her mother's mouth tighten at the corners and knew Teresa, by some unfailing instinct, had got it right.

'Don't be silly, darling, we can easily get that fixed,' Nicola replied firmly. 'Actually, it looks much better on the inside. And it's a nice quiet road. You'll be able to ride your bike around, won't you, Helen?'

Helen, appealed to, nodded quickly, but Teresa was not to be stopped so easily.

'There's no need to sound quite so much like an estate agent. We've bought it, so I suppose we're stuck with it. I suppose you remembered to bring the key?'

'Of course I have,' her mother retorted, offended. 'It's in my bag, somewhere.' She began to search through it, calmly at first. 'I *know* I brought it with us.'

'Try your jacket pocket,' Teresa advised, then as her mother persisted with her frantic rummaging, she reached over and felt inside the jacket pocket for herself.

'Told you,' she said, coolly fishing it out. 'Come on, let's get it over with.' She preceded them across the road and in the narrow gateway to open the door.

The hall was small, so cramped they had to stand in single file, staring up at the steep uncarpeted stairs.

'I like the wallpaper,' Helen said, fingering it.

'It's like an Indian restaurant,' said Teresa

incredulously. 'Crimson and gold. That's what I call subtle.'

'It was an Indian family who had it before us,' Nicola said.

'That explains the smell,' Teresa said, adding quickly as her mother glared at her, 'Of incense, I mean. It's the one nice thing about it, so far.'

'When we have time, we'll redecorate,' Nicola said. 'It'll be something fun to do in the summer holidays. You can each have a vote about the colour.'

Teresa grunted, unmollified, and pushed open the living room door. She let out a yelp of disbelief.

'But there's only one room downstairs! How am I supposed to do my piano practice?'

'The same way as now, on a piano,' her mother replied tartly. 'We're the ones that'll suffer. We won't be able to watch television.'

'Rubbish, you'll have the portable up in your bedroom,' Teresa said accusingly. It was a sore point; her mother hardly ever allowed her to borrow it, and all her friends at school had their own.

They trooped into the living room and walked about, their sandals making echoing noises on the bare boards.

'It was a bit mean of them to take all the carpets,' said Teresa.

'You should have seen them,' her mother smiled. 'I don't think they were our style exactly.'

'Neither is any of this,' Teresa said, staring round at the yellowing walls.

Helen had gone over to the back window. 'I wish —' she said, and stopped.

'You wish what, darling?'

'Oh, nothing.' She couldn't say it. It was Teresa's job to say things. She stared out at the paved yard and the high brick walls in silence.

Her mother came over and put an arm round her shoulders. 'We can have some pots,' she said. 'We can have a row of geraniums on the windowsill, and tubs of sweet peas.'

'And a clematis up the wall,' Helen said with an effort.

But she didn't want tubs and pots. She wanted a garden.

Teresa had gone into the kitchen, which led straight off the living room without a door. She poked in the cupboards and tried the taps.

'Not much wrong there, Tess,' her mother said, coming in behind her. Her voice sounded odd and echoey in the empty room.

'But it's so *small*,' Teresa said. 'Where are we going to sit to eat? Where's everything going to go?'

'We can't bring everything, obviously,' Nicola said quickly. 'That's one of the things you'll have to help me with, Tess, you've got such a good eye. And of course we'll have to measure everything up. But I thought, provisionally, that the sofa could go in the bay window, and the dining-room table could go *here* –'

'Mum, can we see upstairs?' Helen interrupted, not very interested in these details.

'Well, but before we do that –' Nicola looked round instinctively and vainly for somewhere to sit. 'I've been meaning to talk to both of you about this.'

The girls moved together instantly. Their mother's voice and look told them something bad was coming.

'There are two bedrooms,' she began in a clear firm tone, 'and you're to have the biggest.'

'Who, Teresa?' Helen protested. 'That's not fair, Mum. She's always getting –'

'No, I mean *you*, both of you. I'm going to have to ask you to be very grown-up about this, and not make a fuss. You see, I could only afford a house with two bedrooms.'

10

She looked at their blank faces, clearly daunted. 'Oh, do I really have to spell it out?' she said hotly. 'I'm afraid you won't be able to have a bedroom each any more. You're going to have to share.'

That surprise announcement took all the pleasure out of going home. As soon as they got there, Teresa ran upstairs to her own room and banged the door. Their mother went out into the garden, probably, Helen guessed, to cry. Helen herself watched television listlessly for ten minutes, then trailed upstairs and flopped down on her bed. That brought no comfort. Everything in her room, the books, the clothes on the back of the chair and on the floor, the half-finished origami and the skateboard, reminded her that soon she would have no territory of her own. All her stuff would be in the same room as Teresa. Teresa would be free to come in and sneer at her shoe boxes full of fossil stones and, possibly valuable, quartz. Teresa would be able to poke in her cupboards and feel under the bed and pull her things out and laugh at them. There would be no protection, no secrets. It was bad enough now. And she would have to put up with all Teresa's stuff, her fluffy animals, her Nigel Kennedy posters, and her temper.

The thought was enough to drive Helen out to sit on the stairs. It was her favourite part of the house now for taking stock, outside everything, yet at the heart of them. She hooked her arm through the balustrade and looked down into the hall. Some of Dad's books were still in the bookcase. She allowed herself, briefly, to remember what it had been like when he was still at home, sitting working at his desk in the front room, from after breakfast till past her bedtime, every day of the year except Sundays and Christmas. She certainly wouldn't have been sitting on the stairs if he was there. While he was working he demanded absolute peace and quiet, or his plots wouldn't come out right. In the evening the television had to be turned down so low that Helen could sometimes hear him coughing through the wall.

Now and then, if the work was going well but he needed to think, they would hear him move across to the piano and slowly pick out a tune. Once Helen had seen tears in her mother's eyes as she stared at the television, listening. If the work was going badly, he came into the living room with a certain look on his face. Helen got out of the way when that happened; you could usually tell if it was going to be serious. It had got serious on the afternoon of her eighth birthday, when he came into the kitchen in the middle of Helen's noisy birthday party. After that, Nicola had always taken the two girls out for celebrations, to a restaurant or the cinema. Neither of them willingly brought friends home. If someone did come round, Helen took them out into the garden or the garage, and if she played upstairs by herself, she played quietly.

All that was over now, and the relief was so great that Helen had not touched the limits of it. She looked down at the books in the bookcase, and tried to piece together what she could recall of that final and terrible row. It was the fault of the books that they had planned to go to Ireland, where they didn't tax writers or something.

Helen had no interest in her father's books, hadn't read one of them, not even the one dutifully dedicated to her. Teresa was the enthusiast, the devotee, who owned her own hardback copies of the Septimus Pym thrillers and took every new one to school to show her friends and the nuns. Helen always winced slightly if an adult made the connection between her name and her father's, not that it happened often, he wasn't so amazingly famous as all that. But he was doing well enough from the books to want to go home to Ireland, where they didn't tax you, and the move had been discussed on and off for as long as Helen could remember. Then, just before Christmas, Dad had gone over to Dublin to do a few signing sessions in Dublin, and he had telephoned to say he was buying a house and the family were to come over *at once*. Mum had said yes, and then she said no.

Dad had come back in a rage that was the more frightening because it was a cold one, and said he was selling the house anyway. That was what had caused the row, which went on and on, becoming more and more violent, till Helen was hiding in the garage, and the police and Dr Brier came. It had ended with Dad's abrupt departure and the sending on of his things, and then had come the lovely months when the tension had been lifted from the house and Helen had allowed herself to hope he wasn't ever coming back. Mum had talked about having to sell the house, but Helen hadn't heeded it, not even when the 'For Sale' board appeared in the garden. She thought it was one of those things that would never happen, like the holiday in America or the time they went to look at caravans.

And now, here they were, about to move. For a few months the house had become a place you could trust, and now they had to lose it. Helen didn't like the look of the future, sharing that horrible small house with Teresa, but she preferred it immeasurably to having to share anywhere with her father. It would be all right, she told herself. Now that it was just the three of them together, even with Teresa it would be all right.

She could hear her mother downstairs now, with the radio on, moving about the kitchen and starting to cook supper. From Teresa's room, simultaneously, came the sound of the Debussy record she played while doing her homework. They were both feeling better, then. Helen got to her feet, and went downstairs.

'Hello there,' said her mother, turning from the sink where she was washing up. 'Feeling better?'

'Mmm,' said Helen non-committally. She sat down at the end of the table that used to be her father's and which was now cluttered with newspapers and letters and things brought home from school. There was a pen lying amongst them, and Helen clicked it off and on, then started to draw snakes along the blank margin of the parish newsletter. It was warm in the kitchen and sounds from the garden drifted in through the open back door. Helen considered her first completed snake, and added a bow tie and a pair of glasses. Then she paused to watch her mother move from sink to stove, tasting and stirring, pushing back her fair hair from her forehead in a gesture so familiar it hardly registered.

Nicola put the plates to warm, then stood leaning against the worktop, thoughts clearly elsewhere. Her tall soft body, clothed in cords and a sweatshirt, still smelt faintly of comfort to Helen, though she rarely now claimed a hug.

Wanting her attention, Helen said abruptly, 'Would you like to stay here, Mum, if we could?'

Nicola jumped slightly, then smiled. 'If we could, I think it would be very nice. I've always liked this house. I'm sorry to lose it.'

'Me too.' Helen inked in the head of another fat snake, and added cautiously, 'It's not going to be easy, you know, sharing with Teresa.'

'I know,' Nicola sighed. 'I wish I could have found a three-bedroom house for the money, but the only one I saw was in shocking condition. I can just imagine what Teresa would have had to say about it if I'd moved us there.'

'I'm sure you did your best,' Helen said. 'Maybe one of us could sleep in the living room. I wouldn't mind.'

Her mother laughed. 'Wouldn't work, I'm afraid, not when your bedtime is the earliest of the three of us.'

So that was that. Helen sighed and spiralled the pen

14

across the pastoral message from Timothy, our bishop.

'What's for supper?' she asked in compensation.

'Spaghetti.'

'Bolognese? Brilliant.'

'Want to give me a hand with it?'

Helen didn't, but she could hardly say so.

'The sauce is all done,' her mother continued, 'but if you fetch the spaghetti, you can cook it.'

'Okay,' said Helen, sighing. She wondered what it would take to convince her mother she wasn't in the least bit interested in learning how to cook. Sliding out of her seat, she went slowly over to the cupboards and opened one at random. 'Which one is it in?'

'Helen Flynn, how long have we lived in this house and you still don't know where anything is kept?'

'That's so's no one will ever ask her to do anything,' Teresa said, coming in behind them.

Helen stuck out her tongue. 'Not true,' she said.

'Sometimes I wonder,' their mother said dryly. 'Top cupboard on the right. No, other side, Lennie, *right*, I said.'

'It was behind all those tins,' Helen said defensively, pulling out the packet of spaghetti and taking it across to her mother by the stove. 'I don't know what you expect me to have, X-ray eyes or something.'

'No, just to listen to what you're told,' Teresa retorted, sitting down at the table and picking up the parish newsletter. 'Whose is this childish scribble, as if I couldn't guess?'

Helen maintained a dignified silence, watching the saucepan of water on the stove which had reached the point of steaming.

'Do we put it in now?' she asked.

'Not yet, it's not really boiling. Teresa, how hungry are you?'

15

'Extremely.'

'Lennie?'

'Double that.'

'Well, let's say half a packet then.' Nicola pushed the packet towards her. 'Go on, I said you were going to do it. You can put it in now.'

Helen had to admit there was something satisfying in feeding the brittle sticks into the water, watching them bend and curl, then batting them down with the wooden spoon.

Her mother adjusted the heat and said, 'Now if we were really doing this properly, I'd go away and leave you to time it and decide when it was ready.'

Helen grinned. 'Yes, but you know better than to trust me, don't you, Mum?'

Teresa pushed away the parish newsletter and yawned. 'How are you going to manage when you leave home? You'll get malnutrition.'

'No, I won't,' Helen said, coming to sit at the other end of the table. 'I'll get vitamin tablets.'

Nicola turned from the stove and said pointedly, 'Finished your homework, Teresa?'

Teresa heaved one of her sighs. 'Yeah, Mum, sure I have. They only give us about six hours a night. I've still got maths and German, and I haven't done my piano yet. God knows how I'm going to manage when I'm sharing with that little moron.' She nodded down the table towards Helen, who scowled at her.

'Teresa,' their mother said with a warning glance, 'it'll be just as bad for Helen as it will be for you.'

'No, it won't!' Teresa stared back at her in angry desperation. 'You know what she's like, Mum. She doesn't do anything except mess about; her room's a tip. And anyway, I need my own space if I'm going to work. I'm sure that's something I get from Dad. I need it, I really do.'

Away to the right, Helen clutched her hand to her brow, overcome with the agonies of the sensitive artist, and silently echoed her, 'I need it, I really do!'

Unfortunately, Teresa whipped round and caught her before her face was back to normal.

'You can stop pulling faces behind my back, you little rat,' she said nastily. 'You think you're so clever, don't you? You're so far down at the bottom of the class, they're having to build an extension.'

'Teresa, that's enough!' Nicola walked over to the table and confronted her. 'I want you to leave Helen alone, all right?'

'I wish I could,' Teresa said bitterly, picking up the parish newsletter again and tearing little bits out of it. 'I don't want to go near her, personally. You're the one that's bought this stupid two-bedroomed house.'

'All right,' said her mother, with an uneven edge to her voice. 'What do you think I should have done?'

Teresa looked at her for a moment. 'You could have waited,' she said coldly. 'There must have been something with three bedrooms somewhere we could have had. We might even have sorted something out with Dad, and been able to stay here, but oh no, you had to do your independent thing.'

Helen, watching her mother's face, was afraid. But Teresa just went on staring at her coolly. For a second, Nicola seemed unable to say anything at all. When she did speak, it was in a tight quiet voice that meant she was very angry.

'Teresa, your father is selling this house over our heads. Yes, I could have gone to a solicitor and fought it, yes, I could have waited, but I had had enough. Do you understand?' She raised her voice. 'I needed for my own sake, and for your sakes, to get out!'

Teresa looked away. In her hands the parish newsletter

was torn to shreds. 'You could have found a better house,' she said sullenly.

'Teresa, there wasn't time! We don't have to stay there.' Her mother's eyes sought out her face, sought to persuade her. 'We're entitled to half the money from this place when it's sold, but we've got to have somewhere to live in the meantime. On my salary, with no maintenance decided, I'm afraid that's all we can afford.'

Teresa sniffed, evidently unconvinced.

Nicola, with barely concealed exasperation, began to snatch things up off the table. 'Where on earth does all this come from?' she demanded crossly. 'I wish you two could get it into your heads that I'm not the only person in this house responsible for keeping things tidy.'

She shoved the newspapers and letters down the side of the breadbin and plonked down the Parmesan.

'You can lay the table, Teresa,' she said. 'At least Helen's made some contribution to this evening's meal.'

Slowly, almost insolently, Teresa got up and sauntered over to the cutlery drawer. 'Is that knives and forks or forks and spoons?' she called over her shoulder.

'You know perfectly well what we have with spaghetti,' said her mother.

Chapter 7

measuring the ...
to take. A...
supper...
do...

When Teresa came home the followin̶̶̶̶ ̶̶̶̶led the living room door, she almost kno̶̶ ̶̶̶̶er mother unconscious. Nicola looked up at her, pushing the hair out of her eyes, and giggled. Teresa sighed.

'All right, Mother,' she said. 'I give up. What are you doing on your hands and knees?'

Nicola got up and tucked her shirt back into her jeans. 'You make it sound so exciting,' she said. 'I was only trying to measure up the carpet to see if it's worth taking to the new house.'

Teresa rolled her eyes to heaven, and put down her school bag. 'I don't suppose you thought of asking Helen to help you.'

'You know what she's like,' Nicola replied defensively. 'I asked her and she said "Mum, in a minute," and disappeared to the bottom of the garden.'

Teresa eyed the metal tape measure wavering along the edge of the skirting board.

'What are you going to do when you get to the sofa?' she demanded. 'Try and poke it along behind, or were you just going to guess?'

Her mother smiled. 'No, I'll move it if you give me a hand.'

'Oh God, all right,' Teresa said unwillingly. 'But you'd better give me the tape measure then. I know what you're like with centimetres.'

An hour later, when Helen came in from the garden to find out about supper, she found the two of them still at it,

19

rniture upstairs and arguing about what
nst her will, Teresa had got interested. Over
she and her mother peered at the figures noted
n on their scraps of paper.

'Are you sure the dining room table's the best to take?
Why not the kitchen table?' Teresa demanded with her
mouth full of omelette.

'Because the dining table's round and it's got that
extension leaf,' her mother said.

'Better shape for that room, and more adaptable,' Teresa
nodded. 'Okay. Shall I come with you on Saturday to the
new place and measure up?'

'Thank you,' said Nicola in surprise. 'That'd be a great
help.'

'I'll come too,' Helen offered, and was annoyed when
nobody thanked her.

After that, Teresa and her mother sat down together
every afternoon when school was over, to make lists of what
needed to be done, and to begin to do it. Officially Teresa
still disapproved of the move; there was a principle
involved, and her mother was, quite simply, wrong. But
by nature she was an organiser, and she hated to see a job
done badly when she could take a hand in it. Helen was
worse than useless, and she didn't rate her mother much
above Helen. Half the rows with Dad had been caused by
her mother forgetting stupid little things like the bread on
a Bank Holiday, or the fact that the library shut early on
Mondays.

But as the days passed she was pleasantly surprised.
Despite that initial silliness, her mother clearly knew what
she was about. They decided together which carpets and
curtains to take, which to leave, and what needed to be
bought. They began to sort through non-essentials to take
to Oxfam, and when the tea chests arrived, they wrapped
up the good china, and started to pack the books. Their

only serious clash came in deciding how much to leave for Stephen Flynn, the girls' father, to dispose of.

'Of course, there are firms which come in and clear houses for you,' Nicola said. 'But there'll hardly be enough left to justify the cost of that. Still, that's his problem. It'll be a change for him to have something real to worry about.'

Teresa said coldly, 'I'm sure he'll manage. Anyway, I'll help him.' She did not like or understand the look that crossed her mother's face.

'I hope he'll appreciate that,' Nicola said.

'Of course he will,' Teresa said with rising anger. 'Of course he will. Just because you and Helen don't –'

'Don't what?' her mother challenged. 'Don't value the poor misunderstood man?'

'Just forget it,' Teresa said thickly.

As soon as possible, she escaped upstairs to her own room. She put on a tape of Shostakovich's Fifth Symphony, turning up the volume to shut the others out, then threw herself down on the floor cushions in the bay window. Of course Mum was entitled to split up from Dad after what he had done to her; Teresa didn't contest that. She was willing to admit, if only to herself, that life at home was much better without him. With Dad, the rules were never fixed. You had to watch him constantly, gauge his mood. Teresa had learnt how to look forward to treats that could be cancelled without explanation, to accept pocket money that varied on a whim, and meals that ended in shouting or worse. She had accepted as normal the way the happiness of the whole house depended on how well his books were going. She had accepted never being able to bring her friends home, never being able to let her hi-fi rip.

What she couldn't, would never forgive, was the way he had treated Mum. Part of her was ready to kill him for

21

that, and yet, and yet – she loved him. Dad had been kind to her. Not often; the moments were so rare she thought she could remember most of them, the praise for her exam results, a record bought unexpectedly, a compliment when he liked the way she had done her hair. He never complained about her playing music the way he complained about the television, though he must have heard it. Teresa had positioned her desk in the same corner as her father's in the room directly below. When she did her homework, she had thought of him working too, and felt close to him. It was one of the hardest things, now he was gone, that she couldn't visualise the room he worked in. He had only written to them from Dublin once, a brief postcard, giving his address. If Teresa tried to imagine where he was and what he was doing, she saw only the empty room downstairs. Giving up the house would make the loss permanent.

After about an hour, she switched off the tape deck and went downstairs. Helen and her mother were watching television, sitting together on the sofa so companionably that Teresa felt a flicker of jealousy. Helen didn't bother to look up from the screen, but Nicola turned and smiled.

'It's just started, you haven't missed anything.'

Teresa sat down in an armchair and rather ostentatiously picked up a magazine. There was silence for a few minutes. Then her mother said, 'Oh, by the way, I thought you might like the curtains from the spare room to have in your bedroom in the new house, you two.'

Teresa stared across at her suspiciously. 'I thought you wanted them.'

'No, you have them,' her mother said. 'The ones from Helen's bedroom will do me fine.'

It was a peace offering, and a generous one. Teresa had been angling for those curtains even before the move. It was far too good an offer to turn down, though accepting it

22

seemed to ensnare her in complicated guilt. She was well aware of her mother's real opinion of Helen's curtains, stupid red things with a pattern of multi-coloured clowns.

'Thank you,' she said stiffly, after a very brief struggle. Privately, she wondered crossly why her mother had to be such a martyr.

When the real packing started, it was Helen's turn to get upset. It was difficult for the others to find her anything useful to do, and when they tried she was so easily distracted and took so long to complete a job, that it was generally quicker for Teresa or her mother to do it themselves. Helen wandered in and out of whatever room they were working in, disturbed by the chaos and unable to amuse herself. She was jealous of Teresa, working so closely with her mother, and it made her childish and wild. She pried into boxes and pulled things about. She booby-trapped the landing, and hurled surprises from the stairs. When her mother shouted and Teresa looked superior, Helen sulked and, finally, burst into tears.

'I want to help, but you won't let me!'

'I've told you what you can do,' her mother said patiently. 'Sort out your collections. Decide what you want to keep and what you don't, and tape up the boxes tightly so we can pack them.'

'But I want to help *you*,' Helen fretted.

'Well, you can't,' Teresa said, not unkindly. 'When you try, you just get in the way.'

Helen's eyes remained on her mother.

Nicola sighed. 'I'm afraid Teresa's right.'

'All right,' Helen said angrily. 'Keep your rotten packing. I'd rather play by myself anyway.'

She slammed out of the door, wondering what to do. She was determined, anyway, not to raise a finger towards sorting her collections. They could do that themselves if they were going to be so horrible. She went down to the end of the hall and poked inside the pocket of a jacket hanging there for a tennis ball she had left. It was cold and drizzling outside, so it wouldn't be much fun playing in the garden, or even the garage. She began to bounce the ball against the hall wall, quietly at first. Then she got interested. The hall was fairly narrow, so it made catching the ball awkward, especially if she threw it at an angle. She tried throwing it up the stairs. It was easy to catch if the ball just bounced down the steps, but every now and then it caught an edge and flew high.

'Helen!' Her mother didn't even bother to come to the door; she was shouting through it.

'I'm never allowed to do *anything!*' Helen shouted back, and threw the ball as hard as she could, in a rage.

There was nothing left to do now but go into the front room. She opened the door quietly — for all she knew there was a law against *this* as well — and went inside. The moving process had turned the room upside down, she saw. There were no curtains up, and the pictures stood against the walls, leaving pale oblongs where they used to hang. The sofa was loaded with cardboard boxes, and half a dozen tea chests stood in the middle of the room. Helen wandered round, examining labels, stroking the dusty tassels of a fallen lampshade.

She had never lingered in the front room before, even when Teresa and her mother were working in it. Months after her father had gone, it remained his room. She stared at his desk, looking too big now without the word processor, just a wastepaper basket perched ridiculously on its dull brown surface.

After a moment she went over to the piano and punched out a scale with one finger. She could play better than that, but she didn't want to. She hated the piano. Teresa still practised, so it must have been different for her, but Helen could never stand the grudging way her father left the room for her, or sometimes even stayed, reading the newspaper at his desk, one leg swinging to show his impatience, tutting at every wrong note.

As she gave the piano a final poke, the door opened suddenly. It was Teresa.

'I hope you're not messing things up in here,' she said, coming over and closing the lid of the piano. 'And you'd better not have touched any of Dad's stuff. He's coming back soon to sort it all out.'

'Well, good for him, then,' Helen said. 'I hope he enjoys himself.'

Teresa watched her, and a peculiar smile came over her face. 'You'll have to see him, you know. There's no getting out of it.'

Helen moved angrily towards the door. 'I'll do what I want,' she said. 'No one can make me do anything.'

'Oh, but they can,' Teresa said. 'It's what happens when people get divorced. You always have to go on seeing the other parent as long as they want to. He'll take us out on trips, he's allowed. You ask Mum if you don't believe me.'

'I certainly will,' Helen said. But she knew, with a sinking feeling, that Teresa was right. She nearly always was.

Chapter Three

The day of the move finally came. It was a school day, shortly before half-term and Nicola had arranged for Teresa to have the day off to help, but nothing could persuade her to let Helen stay.

She got the two girls up half an hour earlier than usual, and when Helen came down into the kitchen she took one look at her mother and knew better than to try to renew the argument. Nicola already looked strained and tired, dressed for action in a baggy old tracksuit, her hair scraped back into a wispy ponytail. She was drinking coffee, cupping the mug in her hands and standing by the sink as if it took longer to drink sitting down.

'Where's everything gone?' Helen asked, looking round at the empty shelves.

'Teresa and I packed it all after you were in bed,' her mother said shortly.

'What, even the cereal?' Helen asked, appalled.

'There's croissants on the table.' Nicola nodded towards the cellophane-wrapped packet. 'You don't need a plate. I'll heat them up for you if you like.'

'No, it's okay,' Helen said, with a bad grace. She thought croissants were overrated at the best of times, and this certainly wasn't one of them.

Teresa came downstairs a minute later, in her jeans. Her mother only seemed properly to wake up on her arrival.

'Cup of coffee, love?' she offered. 'And you'd better eat something. It's going to be a long morning.'

'Telling me,' Teresa said.

Helen eyed Teresa jealously as she sat down opposite and bit into a croissant. She hadn't bothered to comb her hair and there were dark circles under her eyes.

'We were up till gone one last night,' she said enthusiastically, with her mouth full. 'Weren't we, Mum?'

'Lucky you,' Helen said sourly. 'What I'd like to know is, how am I going to get home tonight? I don't know the way.'

'Teresa will come and pick you up,' her mother said. 'Now, if you've had all you want to eat, can you please get your things together quickly. I don't want to have to chase you this morning, when we've got so much to do. The removal men are supposed to be here by nine, and there's all the bedding to pack, and the things in the bathroom.'

Helen slouched off her chair, not bothering to finish her croissant. She would be miles early for school if she had to set off now. They were turning the whole day into something horrible. She went upstairs for her school bag and came down again, bumping it on every step.

Her mother came out into the hall. 'It'll be nice when you see it this evening,' she said. 'It'll be just like home.'

Put that way, it didn't sound too bad. Helen surreptitiously wiped her eyes on the back of her hand and said, 'So when will Teresa be coming?'

Teresa stuck her head round the door. 'Quarter to four, when you finish,' she said. 'But wait at the playing field entrance, not near the road, okay? It's quicker if we don't have to walk round.'

'Okay,' Helen agreed.

'Have a good day,' her mother said, and Teresa smiled. But Helen felt quite miserable as she shut the front door and set off down the street.

At a quarter to four she was waiting impatiently outside the school, straining her eyes for any sign of Teresa. The stream of boys and girls in navy blue pouring out through the gates made it difficult to see anyone coming the other way. One or two girls from her class stopped to chat, and Sean McAnespie tried in a friendly way to run her over with his bicycle, but after they had gone there was nothing to break the tension. As the crowd coming through the gates started to thin out, Helen saw other children waiting for parents arriving in cars. The cars came and went; the flood of uniforms heading round the side of the building towards the gate was reduced to the merest trickle, and still there was no sign of Teresa. Helen could see right down to the bottom of the road now, and Teresa wasn't there.

The first of the teachers emerged from the school and started walking towards the car park. Helen lowered her head, scared in case someone would notice her, come over, and ask what was wrong. It wouldn't do any good, she would just look stupid. She couldn't be sure she had remembered the number of the house properly, she wasn't sure exactly where it was, or how to get there.

None of that mattered if Teresa was coming, but where was Teresa? Suddenly, Helen's stomach turned over. Teresa must have had an accident. It was the obvious thing: she was so impatient crossing the road, dashing between the cars while Helen shouted, 'Don't!' and had to wait, fretting, for the lights to change. If Teresa had been hit by a car, nobody would know. She could be lying in a hospital ward somewhere, with the nurses ringing and ringing the old phone number and getting no answer. Probably it had already been cut off by now. Nobody would know. Poor old Teresa. But at least if she was in hospital, she was being taken care of. Helen was starting to worry about herself now. In a minute or two, if nothing happened, she would have to decide what to do.

'Well, I'm not asking a teacher,' she said stubbornly, out loud. She would just have to go and find the house herself. It was only a question of deciding when to give up and move on. But what on earth would Mum say when she came back on her own? That is, if she did manage to find the house . . .

'For God's sake, Helen, what are you doing standing over there like a moron? I've been waiting for you for ages!'

It was Teresa, of course. She was coming round the side of the building at top speed, looking furious. Helen's immense relief on seeing her was quickly converted into resentment. There was no need for her to look so angry; she was the one that was late. Unless —

'I told you to wait near the playing field, not here,' Teresa said. 'I might have known you wouldn't listen.'

'I *did* listen,' Helen said, picking up her bag. 'I just didn't remember, that's all.'

Teresa let out an impatient groan which modified, on a closer look at Helen, into a noise of derision. 'You were frightened,' she said incredulously. 'You thought something had happened.'

'No, I didn't,' Helen retorted defensively, but Teresa wasn't fooled.

'You thought I'd died or something. What a plank!'

She set off immediately back round the school, leaving Helen, mutely indignant, no choice but to follow.

As they crossed the playing field to the main road, Teresa started again.

'I bet you don't even know where we're going.'

''Course I do.'

'Where, then?'

'The new house, stupid.'

'Ha-ha, very amusing,' Teresa said. 'Which way do we go at the bottom of this road, then, if you're so clever.'

'Left,' hazarded Helen.

'You only guessed,' Teressa said grudgingly, and

ducked between the parked cars to cross the road.

She looked older out of her uniform, Helen thought, trailing after her. She could be sixteen. It was partly Teresa's face, scornful and alert under the reddish fringe, partly, of course, her figure, more pronounced in jeans and t-shirt than in the convent tunic. Helen didn't know whether to be jealous or not. She thought she would despise herself if she ever got like Teresa, if she started to worry about eating chocolate and what boys thought of her.

'Now pay attention to where we're going,' Teresa said in a hectoring tone. 'We turn right here, at the post office, and then left at that next corner.'

Helen looked, dutifully. The post office was in a short row of shops, and when they turned round the corner they were opposite the British Legion Club. A man in a blazer with a shiny red face and thin white hair stood on the steps with a glass in his hand, watching them as they passed.

'I know where we are,' Helen said. 'This is the way we come to church.'

'Wow, aren't you clever?' Teresa retorted, with automatic sarcasm. 'Yup, there it is, coming up on the right. Good old Seggy Heart.'

Helen turned her head away as they passed the church, focussing her eyes on the garage across the street. The statue inside the church railings always embarrassed her. There was something indecent about Jesus standing there exposing his heart with that soft look on his face, something almost shaming.

She wished they had called the church after something else, a saint, maybe, or even the Holy Family, like the church near Teresa's school.

'And then it's next right, do you see?' Teresa continued. 'If we kept straight on, we'd eventually hit the sea front.'

The street they turned into, Helen noted for future

reference, was called Queen Street. The front doors opened straight onto the pavement, but she quite liked the lace curtains and the ornaments in the windows. She was too afraid of Teresa's mockery to comment on them to her.

'What's our house like?' she asked instead. 'Does it look okay now all our own stuff is unpacked?'

'Sure, on the inside,' Teresa said. 'It's still a crap place to have to live.'

They walked on in silence. Then, when they reached another corner, Helen knew suddenly where they were.

'This is Arthur Street,' she said. 'This is it.'

'Yup.'

It wasn't as nice as Queen Street, Helen thought despondently, in spite of the houses having front yards. They were all so dingy and sort of broken-down looking. They passed a boy in a dirty t-shirt, leaning against one of the low front walls. He stared after them and burst into sudden violent laughter.

'Frizzlehead!'

Helen stopped and turned round, but Teresa pulled her back.

'Come on, forget it. They've called you worse things at school sometimes, haven't they?'

'School's school,' Helen said. 'This is supposed to be home.'

'And speaking of which –' Teresa waved her hand in a grand gesture. 'The Maison Flynn. Try not to throw up.'

To Helen's relief it looked better than she remembered. The paintwork was a little smarter than the two houses on either side, and the curtains in the windows were familiar. There was a neat stack of flattened cardboard boxes beside the front door, which Teresa opened and went through.

'We're back,' she called up the stairs.

Nicola appeared on the landing. She looked hot and irritated; her hair was messed up and her tracksuit was

31

dusty white, as if she had been hugging a wall.

'I'm almost finished,' she called down. 'Put the kettle on, will you, Tess, and make us all some coffee?'

'Okay.'

Teresa went into the downstairs room. Helen looked up at her mother's weary face, hesitated, and followed suit.

It was strange to see the furniture from different rooms re-combined here in one.

'Not bad, is it?' Teresa came in from the kitchen. 'It took us absolutely ages to unpack. We didn't stop for lunch, just got sandwiches from the newsagent's. I'll show you where that is tomorrow. It's the nearest place for buying sweets and stuff.'

Helen went slowly round the room. The bookcase and the table from the dining room were nearest the kitchen, and on the other side of the room the sofa was in the bay window with the armchairs opposite. The piano was crammed in behind the door.

'There's not a lot of room,' she said doubtfully.

'Oh, I don't know,' said Teresa, still flushed with the pride of a job well done. 'Look on the bright side. We'll be able to watch telly while we're eating.'

Helen didn't think Mum would allow that. She sat down in an armchair, and tried to see how the room looked from various angles.

'What on earth are you doing, Helen?' her mother demanded irritably, coming in. 'If you want to do yoga, do it on the floor.'

Helen righted herself. 'I was only —'

'Never mind. Just don't do it.' Nicola sat down on the sofa and let out a groan. 'Oh, that's better. What I need is a long hot bath. Still, it didn't go too badly, did it, Tess? Only two glasses broken and a chip out of the piano.'

'And that wasn't even us, that was the removal men,' said Teresa, coming in with the coffee. 'I hope you didn't want one, Helen, because I didn't make you one.'

'That's okay,' Helen said. She wasn't very keen on hot drinks. 'I'm going upstairs anyway.'

Teresa, who had just sat down, immediately rose to her feet.

'Hold on,' said Nicola wearily. 'Teressa, you're not taking that cup upstairs and leaving it somewhere to get stone cold. Helen's perfectly entitled to go upstairs on her own. It's her room as well, remember.'

'But I want to show her where everything is,' Teresa protested. 'So she'll know which bits are mine and which are hers. I don't want her poking around in my things, Mum! You've got to make her wait for me.'

'I haven't *got* to do anything,' Nicola retorted. 'If Helen wants to wait for you, that's fine, but I'm not forcing her.'

'I'll wait,' Helen said. There was no point in getting Teresa in too much of a state. She only took it out on you afterwards.

Teresa sat down again and began to drink her coffee in quick angry slurps. Helen wandered over to the piano. The broken piece was lying on top, and she amused herself trying to fit the long jagged splinter back onto the lid where it had been snapped off. However well you glued it, the line would always show. Behind her, her mother put on the television and, turning round automatically, Helen was surprised to see her lying stretched out on the sofa, dusty trainers up on the arm. It was something she would never have let them do.

'You'll ruin that sofa,' Teresa said sepulchrally from the depths of her chair.

'It's mine to ruin,' Nicola retorted. She lay back even further, and put her arms behind her head. 'This is my house,' she said in a tone of luxurious wonder. 'No one else's. I decide what happens here.'

The two girls looked at her in silence.

'What's for supper?' Helen asked eventually, with a feeling of smoothing things back to normal.

Her mother laughed. 'Fish and chips,' she said. 'One of you can fetch it from that place round the corner. I'm doing no more tonight, not even the washing-up. And before you ask, Teresa, no, there isn't any salad in the fridge.'

'I know,' said Teresa, annoyed. 'I helped you move it, remember?'

'Let's go upstairs,' Helen said, pacifically. 'You can show me where everything is.'

'Chuck me a cushion, one of you, will you, before you go?' Nicola said. 'Thanks.'

In the bedroom, Teresa took immediate charge.

'We put your bed by the window because you go to bed earlier than me, all right? And we unpacked your clothes, but we left everything else, books and stuff, for you to do.'

Helen went over to the cardboard boxes in the middle of the room, but before she started putting things away she had a good look round. It was all right, she supposed. There just wasn't very much room, with two beds and all the furniture. Teresa had already covered the wall above her bed with posters, but because of the window, there wasn't a lot of room above Helen's bed for hers. She started to sling paperbacks into her bookcase while she considered an appeal to Mum.

Teresa lolled on her bed, watching. 'Okay if I put some music on?'

'S'pose so.'

The music welled into the room, something slow and gloomy sounding that Helen didn't know.

'Mum was a bit funny downstairs just now, wasn't she?' Teresa asked.

Helen sat back on her heels and looked at her. 'I don't

know. Was she?'

'Oh, you never want to say anything against her,' Teresa said with scorn. 'You know full well what I mean. All that stuff about it being *her* house. It's ours just as much. If she starts going all funny, all *Guardian* Women's page –'

'What do you mean?'

'Oh, you know. "I never truly found myself until I left my husband and eight children and started an Open University course in basket weaving".'

'She's not going to leave us,' Helen said uncertainly. 'Not with him.'

'Don't be so pathetic, Lennie! I didn't mean it literally. Not that I'd mind being left with him.' Honesty compelled her to add, 'Well, for part of the time, anyway.'

But Helen only stared at her in horror.

'Oh, you're so *brainwashed!*' Teresa bounced on her bed in exasperation. 'Look, I'm not saying Dad was okay, far from it, but it takes two to make a mess like they made. We've done stuff about psychology in school. People like Dad need special circumstances, they need to be understood. If Mum had only been a bit more tolerant, if she didn't always have to be right –'

'I don't think landing in hospital makes her right,' Helen said coldly. 'I think it makes her scared.'

'You're the one that was scared,' Teresa said with a peculiar smile. 'Mum told me it had gone on too long for her to be scared. It had happened too often. That's exactly what she said, Lennie, so you needn't look at me like that. And all I want to know is, okay, if it was so terrible, if she hated him so much, why didn't she leave earlier, when we were babies? Why didn't she leave after you were born?'

Helen didn't want to listen to this any more. She turned her back on Teresa and got on with her unpacking. 'Ask Mum,' she said over her shoulder. 'Don't ask me. Ask her.'

'I will,' Teresa said. But she made no move to go

downstairs. She went on watching Helen from over the foot of her bed. 'Mum didn't leave because of herself,' she said. 'She left because of you.'

Helen got up. 'I don't want to talk to you any more,' she said coldly. 'I'm going downstairs.'

'Go on then,' Teresa jeered. 'Run to Mum like you always do. But she'll tell you herself, if you ask her. It's what she told me. She left Dad because of your nightmares and wetting the bed and refusing to go to school, all that stuff, and not because of anything that happened to her.'

Helen hung on to the door. 'Are you saying it's my fault?'

'If you like.' Teresa was smiling that strange smile again.

'Then I'm glad!' Helen shouted, and slammed the door.

Chapter Four

The following evening, Helen was alone with her mother in the living room of the new house. Teresa was out at ballet and wouldn't be back for another hour at least. Supper was over, and Nicola was sitting at one end of the sofa marking history essays. She was wearing a pale blue shirt and white trousers, which Helen, lolling on the floor in front of the television, thought made her look particularly summery and nice.

She was satisfied with everything that evening; it was Friday and the whole weekend stretched ahead, full of possibilities. There was no need to rush to do anything. She hadn't bothered to change out of her uniform, and her school bag still lay where she had dumped it, just inside the door. She lay on the carpet, half watching television, half playing with some dice she had found while unpacking. Her mother made little noises of despair or surprise and scribbled in the margins of her essays, and neither of them felt the need to talk for quite a while.

'Got a lot of homework this weekend?' Nicola asked eventually, removing the red pen from her mouth and taking a swig of coffee.

'Mmm,' said Helen vaguely. She gathered the dice into her hands for another throw.

'Like what, for instance?'

'Oh, a mariner's map for history and some vocab for a French test.'

'Well don't try and learn it in front of the telly on Sunday evening like you usually do,' Nicola said, putting some severity into her voice. 'How about if I test you on it on Sunday afternoon?'

'I do it the proper way, actually,' Helen informed her. 'Mrs Fox says the best way to learn vocabulary is to keep coming back to it, not sitting down and trying to memorise it all in one go. Anyway, she's very sympathetic if we get things wrong.'

'I'm not sure I like the sound of that,' Nicola said wryly. 'I haven't been at all sympathetic to my lot and their awful essays.'

'That's because they're older,' Helen said blithely. She rolled onto her stomach and contemplated her mother. 'I wouldn't mind being in your class.' Nicola laughed. 'Maybe you should consult Teresa about that,' she said. 'She loathed being in my class when I was her form teacher at the convent, remember? No wonder she opted for biology instead of history, poor girl.'

'But that's only because all the clever ones are expected to pick science,' Helen said. 'And Teresa has to be top, or she feels miserable.'

'Unlike you, of course,' Nicola looked at her ruefully. She pushed the essays to one side, and patted the sofa beside her. 'You know, we're going to have to have a serious talk about your school work. Now we're properly settled, I don't want any more of those notes coming home about you losing books, and not working in class, and your mysterious absences from domestic science class. Now we're here in a house by ourselves, you've got a chance to get on. There shouldn't be anything to hold you back now, should there?'

'No,' said Helen, watching the dice roll across the carpet.

'I'm serious, Lennie,' her mother said gently. 'I think you could do just as well as Teresa if you tried. You've just decided not to try. I think we both know the reason, but

38

that reason's gone now, hasn't it? All the way to Ireland. It needn't affect you any more, not if you don't want it to.'

Helen hunched her shoulders, looked away and waited for her mother to stop. She wished they wouldn't all keep going on about it, her mother, Teresa, the teachers at school; it didn't do any good. Always they said she could be just as good as Teresa, if she tried. But who wanted to be like Teresa? No one in their right mind.

After a moment she heard her mother sigh and reach for the essays again. Helen picked up one of her dice and began to examine it closely.

'Mum,' she said. 'Just why did you and Dad split up?'

Her mother didn't reply at once and to Helen it seemed as if the whole room went very quiet. She turned the dice in her fingers, listening to the sound of her own breathing. Then her mother said, 'Oh, it's simple, really. He liked me, but he didn't love me, and I loved him but I didn't like him.'

Helen tossed the dice up in the air, caught it, and put it in her pocket. She didn't exactly understand, but it was convincing.

'Mum,' she said, twisting to look at her, 'do you *like* Teresa?'

Nicola smiled. 'Why, don't you?'

But Helen couldn't start telling her about Teresa, because Teresa was back.

The slam of the front door announced her return. She came in, short plait bouncing, her face reddened by some strong emotion.

'You're driving me to ballet next week, Mother,' she announced.

Her mother looked at her, perplexed. 'But it's only ten minutes' walk, Tess. You used to get the bus from the old house. It'll still be light – '

Teresa threw down her bag and flung herself onto a

39

chair. Her pink tights under her school coat made her legs look fat, and she pulled down the coat with an automatic gesture.

'I'm not having people laughing at me,' she said. 'This bloody area! Two girls yelled after me, 'You've lost your tutu!' and a boy offered to show me his jock strap.'

Nicola half rose in concern. 'Teresa, he didn't — '

'No, of course not,' Teresa said impatiently. 'I told him to — to get lost,' she amended it quickly. 'But they were laughing at me, the plebs. Even the grown-ups were staring at my tights.' She tugged at her coat again. 'God, I hate it round here. And what about all that hassle yesterday evening, when Helen went out on her bike? She wasn't doing anything, and she got picked on.'

Helen didn't want to be reminded of that. She had gone out after supper, intending to find the newsagent Teresa had told her about. She turned down the first alley she came to, and a couple of boys ran into her path and pushed her off her bike. She scraped her elbow in the fall, and the only thing that kept her from crying was sheer anger, seeing that big teenager riding off on her bike with his knees up round his ears, and his friend running after him yelling, 'Give us a go, Kev!' They had found the bike later that evening, Mum and she, abandoned in another alley with the chain off. It was out in the yard now; she hadn't felt like riding it today.

'I'm sorry, love, it's rotten,' Mum was saying now to Teresa. 'But they'll get used to seeing you.'

'You mean I'll have to get used to being laughed at,' Teresa said bitterly. She picked up her bag to go upstairs.

'Well, I don't even know if we'll be able to afford to keep the car,' Nicola said. 'Look, I'll take you to ballet next week anyway. How's that?'

'Don't bother,' said Teresa crossly. 'I'll manage. They're just so *stupid*, that's all.

Nicola got to her feet. 'You go and get changed,' she said. 'Then I think we all need something to cheer ourselves up. Let's walk down to the shops and get a video.'

'Oh, brilliant,' said Helen. 'Can we make some popcorn?'

'I don't see why not,' her mother smiled. 'Does that suit you, Teresa?'

'I suppose,' said Teresa gracelessly. 'So long as it isn't anything with Arnold Schwarzenegger. And it's my pick, because Helen chose last time.'

The next day was Saturday. Helen woke early and, tweaking back the curtains, saw that it was a fine sunny day. She went downstairs in her pyjamas. Her mother was at the table, eating toast and coffee, with a newspaper propped up beside her plate. Stopping to refold it with buttery fingers, she looked up at Helen and smiled.

'You're up early, Lennie. Planning anything special?'

'Depends.' Helen sat down and helped herself to cereal. 'Is Teresa going shopping with you?'

'I expect so. She usually comes and reads the backs of all the packets before I'm allowed to buy them.'

'In that case, can I have my pocket money now?' Helen asked. 'I want to go down to the sea front.'

'Sure, if you can find my purse,' her mother said. 'Only don't spend it all in an arcade, will you? You need something for the collection tomorrow.'

Helen made quick work of breakfast, then dug up Nicola's purse from down the side of the sofa. She extracted her pocket money and charged back upstairs to get dressed. As she threw open the bedroom door, a leg waved irritably from under the duvet on Teresa's bed.

'For God's *sake*,' her voice came out in a muffled explosion. 'Some of us are still trying to sleep.'

41

'Sorry,' Helen whispered. But she couldn't help making more noise when she accidentally knocked a book onto the floor, and yet again when she was groping for one of her sandals under the bed. As she stood up, sandal in hand, Teresa threw back her duvet and sat up. Her hair was all spiky and bunched and the side of her face was marked with little red wavy creases from her pillow. She glared at Helen without speaking, set her feet in her fluffy slippers, and shuffled across to the door.

'Mum wants you to go shopping with her, anyway,' Helen called after Teresa guiltily. Then she sat down to put on her sandals and forgot all about it.

Once out of the house, Helen felt extraordinarily alive. The sky above her was high and blue, with clouds moving briskly across it. In shadow the pavement was almost chilly, so she crossed the street to catch the sun, lifting her face to enjoy the mixture of breeze and warmth. It heightened her pleasure to feel the coins in her pockets, but the greatest feeling of all was the absence of worry about what might be happening at home while she was out.

She reached the sea front in a few minutes, and stopped to sniff the air. A mingled smell of chips and hot dogs and boiling sugar came from the cafés and shops further along the front, but the wet salt smell of the beach came from just opposite. Helen ran across the road, scrambled onto the sea wall and jumped, plunging into the cold dry sand below. She got to her feet again, brushed herself down, and began to walk.

The dry sand was in shadow, and pleasantly cool for her sandalled toes at first, but her calf muscles soon got tired and she took a diagonal course out onto the ribbed wet sand. The foamy pools and bright feathery seaweed meant, she guessed, that the tide was going out. Beyond the far

42

edge of the sand lay the rocks, flat and shiny brown, fringed with ribbony weed. Beyond the rocks, lapping at them in the distance, was the sea.

The beach was almost empty. Helen stopped, hands on hips, to take in the wide shallow curve of it. A long way off, a man was throwing a ball to his dog and a gang of boys were playing around a sewage pipe. From the holiday caravans at Warren's Point to the receding green headland at the other end of the bay, those were the only people she could see. Helen was happy. She picked up a small white stone, put it in her pocket, and walked on.

When she left the beach at last, it was to cross the road to the row of shops from which wafted a most delicious smell of hot mint. It came from The Rock Shop, through whose window she could see two women in white coats operating a machine that pulled out the rock in long soft strands, stretching and folding it like gum. The shop also sold humbugs, cinder toffee and chocolate crunch. Helen fingered the money in her pocket thoughtfully before moving on.

Next door was the Italian café they sometimes came to in the summer as a treat after shopping in town. Helen paused for a moment to listen to the whoosh of the hot milk coming out of the cappuccino machine. The ice-cream here, she knew, was delicious, but more than she was prepared to pay out of her limited pocket money.

On the other side of the café was the amusement arcade, where she had been intending to spend her money all along. She stood in the doorway for a moment, peering in; there was sometimes a man there to make sure only adults came in, but this time there was no one. Helen took a breath and went inside. The air was stale, smelling of cigarettes and dirty carpets, and the dark interior was animated only by the flashing lights and cartoon noises of the machines. There were few people playing them, so early in the morning. Helen stood by a middle-aged man for a while, watching him feed in coin after coin like an automaton. She herself was a cautious player. She liked to go from machine to machine, watching other people play, pressing the credit buttons and weighing her chances before she ever risked a coin. She never left an amusement arcade penniless, unlike Teresa, who had once wasted three pounds of her birthday money trying to win a jackpot.

There was a girl about Teresa's age, playing a machine right at the back. Helen went over to her and watched her. She was playing with a fierce kind of desperation, smoking and swearing and punching the buttons of the machine. Helen wondered if the wailing toddler in the pushchair beside her could possibly be her own. His t-shirt was covered in bits of crisp and he was flailing his arms and bucking his body as if he was trying to get out of the safety harness. Leaning sideways, Helen saw that his crisp packet had fallen out of the pushchair onto the dirty carpet. It made her feel uncomfortable; why wasn't the girl taking any notice? Helen glanced at her, stooped quickly, and restored the crisps to the little child. His crying cut out like a stopped tape, and instantly the girl turned round and said fiercely, 'Whassamatter?' and then, with indifference, 'Oh, ta.'

As the girl turned back to the machine, Helen moved away. She felt unhappy, rather sickened. She wanted to get out, back into the air and the light. She made for the door and, as she turned, the pound coin she was holding slipped out of her fingers and rolled along the carpet near her feet. Helen crouched down to track it; to her relief she saw something gleaming at the foot of a video machine. She moved quickly, but not quickly enough. A dirty trainer came crashing down on her money. Helen stopped dead. Her eyes travelled up baggy jeans and faintly printed t-shirt to the face. It was the boy who had taken her bike.

It was Kev.

'Prove it's not mine,' he said hoarsely. 'Prove I didn't drop it.'

'You know it's not yours,' Helen said. 'Look.' She showed him her remaining money. 'I only get one pound twenty-five pocket money, and I haven't spent any of it yet.'

But Kev only laughed. 'That'll stand up in court, won't it? Got your name and address on the back, I bet.' He pretended to snatch the other money out of her hand. 'Go on, piss off before you lose it all.'

Helen was too angry now to be careful. 'You're not having my money,' she said. 'I'm going to tell —' But there wasn't anyone she could tell, not without leaving him alone with the money.

Kevin was smiling now, showing yellow-white teeth in a grin that split his freckled face. 'I know who you are,' he said. 'You're from that family that's just moved into Arthur Street, the ones with the posh accents and the clapped-out Renault Five. I pinched your bike.'

'We found it,' Helen retorted, hitching up her chin. 'I got it back.'

'I'd have kept it if it had been any good,' Kev said. 'But it was crap, like your car.'

'Our car is not crap!'

But Kev had got bored with the conversation. He suddenly pushed Helen out of the way and picked up the pound.

'Ta,' he said, still grinning. 'I'll be able to buy ten fags with this. I'll think of you while I smoke them.'

'You won't, you know,' said a voice behind them.

As Kev turned round, Helen saw who it was that had spoken. He had been playing one of the machines near them, apparently indifferent to what had been happening. Now, as Kev faced him, he held out one brown hand.

45

'Give the little girl her money back.'

Kev slewed round to look at Helen, then back again at his challenger. 'It's my money she's trying to pinch off me,' he said. 'I dropped it, and she said —'

'Ten out of ten for imagination,' the man said, smiling. 'The only trouble is, I was listening. So unless you want me to drag you to the manager and get you permanently banned —'

Kev swore and flung the money down on the floor. 'My dad says you Pakis should go back where you came from,' he said. 'And take your Kattomeat curries with you.'

'Educated man, your dad. Has he learnt to read and write yet?'

Kev swore again and pushed past the man, deliberately banging into him on his way to the door. 'I know where you live, you Paki bastard,' he called back. 'You're going to get something very nasty through your letter box one of these days.'

'What, you mean a poll tax demand?' retorted the man.

Kev swore again, and walked away.

The man grinned at Helen and picked up the pound at his feet. 'Sorry about that,' he said. 'Some people are sore losers.'

'Thank you very much for helping me,' Helen said. I'm sorry he called you all those things.'

'Don't worry.' He dropped the pound into her hand. 'I grew up in London. I can't take the kids round here very seriously. They're all mouth, know what I mean?'

He turned and picked up a carrier bag of shopping from next to the fruit machine. 'Shall we get out of here? You really don't want to waste that money now you've got it back.'

Outside, Helen got a proper look at her rescuer. He must have been about twenty or so, not very tall, but quite strong-looking. He was wearing white cotton jeans with big turn-ups, and an orange grandad shirt that showed the muscles of his neck and shoulders. Helen felt rather shy of him. There were Asian boys in her school, but apart from shopkeepers she had never spoken to a grown-up.

His eyes, behind small gold-rimmed glasses, met hers with warm curiosity. 'So what were you doing in there?'

'Same as you, I expect,' Helen said, a little crossly. She didn't want to be told off.

'Yes, but if I lose a pound on a machine, I've got a few more, whereas you have to go without goodies for the rest of the week,' he said, grinning. He had a nice grin, his teeth white against his dark brown skin.

He eased a cigarette packet out of his pocket, caught Helen's frown, and shoved it back. 'So which way are you heading?' he asked.

'Home,' said Helen cautiously.

'Same here,' he said with absurd delight. 'That means we can go together, doesn't it?'

'Don't be silly,' Helen said pettishly. 'I haven't told you where I live, and I'm not supposed to talk to strangers.'

'Tell you what. I live in Henry Street. If you live anywhere near there, we can walk together. If not — '

'That's just round the corner from us,' Helen said in surprise.

'Well, why don't you walk me back? That way, if that — Kevin, was it? — comes back and tries anything, you can protect me.' He hunched up his shoulders and looked fearfully round in a way that made Helen laugh.

'All right,' she said. 'I'll come with you as far as Henry Street.'

They set off together, walking fairly slowly because of the man's heavy shopping.

'It's funny, I haven't seen you around,' he said after a moment. 'I thought I knew most of the local kids by sight.'

'We've just moved in,' Helen said. 'Last Thursday, as a matter of fact.'

'Great!' He seemed genuinely pleased. 'You picked the right part of town. Some bits are really posh and boring, like those big houses off St Anne's Road. Nobody knows their neighbours, and nothing ever happens.'

When Helen did not reply, he glanced down at her in surprise.

'We used to live near there,' she said in a small, cold voice.

'Oopsie,' said the man, glancing round him as if for rescue. After a minute he started again.

'Well, I'm probably wrong about it being boring over there,' he said. 'But I certainly like our bit better.'

'I don't,' said Helen. She started to tell him what had happened to her bike.

He nodded impatiently and eventually broke in. 'I know, I know, pain in the neck, isn't it? There's always a few creeps who want to spoil things for everyone else. But there's a lot more going for the place than you've seen so far. At least it's alive, do you get me? There's such a mixture of people. There's the students, like me — ' he flashed his grin at her. 'There's the alternatives and squatters, people like that. There's the Muslims, the Pakistanis and whatever. And there's the ordinary English. It's great.'

Helen was unconvinced, and looked it.

'You'll like it when you get older,' he said confidently.

'My sister's fourteen, and she hates it,' Helen said.

'What's she then, a Young Conservative?'

'No,' said Helen. 'She's just normal.'

It looked for a moment as though they were going to quarrel seriously. The man's eyebrows knitted together and he opened his mouth to say something sharp. Then, abruptly, to Helen's relief, he let out a sigh instead. 'It's no good.' He looked at her, and his face relaxed. 'We can't quarrel properly until we've been introduced. I'm Velsford, Velsford Fernandes.'

'Sorry?'

'Velsford,' he repeated. Helen could see that if she wasn't careful, he would start to get angry again.

'That's an unusual name,' she said cautiously. 'Is it Indian?'

'Certainly not.' He lifted his chin. 'It's Goan.' He glanced at her puzzled face and grinned. 'Now I suppose you're going to tell me you've never heard of Goa.'

Helen hated to have to admit it. 'We haven't done many actual countries in geography,' she said. 'Only sort of themes, like water, and recycling.'

Velsford nodded in an 'I might have guessed it,' sort of way. 'Goa's in India now, but it isn't India, not really. It belonged to the Portugese for hundreds and hundreds of years.'

'Is your accent Portugese, then?' Helen asked with interest. It had been puzzling her since the first time he spoke. It wasn't local, but nor was it like the accents of the older Asians she had listened to.

Velsford tried not to laugh, but he clearly couldn't help it. 'It's North London,' he said. 'That's where I grew up, in sunny Edmonton.'

'So you were born here?' Helen was rather disappointed.

''Fraid so. My dad's family got kicked out of Uganda by Idi Amin, so they came over here.'

'Why, what had they done?'

'Opened a shop,' said Velsford, and shrugged. 'Crazy world, isn't it?'

They were passing the Bangladeshi mosque, which was just a shop front with curtains across the windows. One of the windows was boarded up with hardboard again.

'So are you a Muslim?' Helen asked. 'There aren't many

at my school, because it's for Catholics mainly, but they gave this presentation at assembly once – '

'Course I'm not Muslim,' Velsford interrupted her. 'My mum goes to mass every day and you're calling me a Muslim?'

Helen couldn't tell if he was really shocked, or just pretending to be. In any case, she gave up on it.

'You should come and meet my mum,' she told him. 'She teaches history, so I'm sure she knows all about the Portugese and everything. If we go home now, I bet you she'll invite you to stay for lunch.'

Velsford looked uncertain.

'Honestly,' Helen nodded. 'She wants to meet new people. She told me so.' She could almost remember her mother saying something like that, so it wasn't a lie. In any case, she really wanted her mother to meet him, to hear what she said. Helen liked him, but he was so strange she couldn't be sure.

'All right,' Velsford's face cleared up. 'Which street is yours, then – no, let me guess. Turner Street?'

'No,' said Helen, and smiled. 'You'll just have to wait and see.'

Chapter Five

At about the same time Helen was confronting Kevin in the amusement arcade, Teresa and her mother arrived back from the supermarket and started to unload the car.

'The post's arrived,' Teresa said, walking round it on her way through into the kitchen, where she dumped the first of the boxes of groceries. Nicola went back out to pick it up.

'Here's a letter from your father for you,' she said, picking it out of the small sheaf of junk mail and re-directed bills. 'Will you mind if I read it after you? I want to have some idea of what he's up to.'

Teresa took the letter and stuck it in the back pocket of her jeans. 'I'll tell you when he says he's coming,' she said shortly.

'Well, but I want to know a bit more than that,' her mother said. 'I'd like to know what sort of state he's in.'

'You mean you care?' Teresa stared at her.

'Teresa —' Her mother raised her arms towards her in appeal, but getting no response, let them fall slowly to her sides. 'I care about how his state affects us,' she said flatly. 'All right? The letters from his solicitor don't make any sense at all.' She pushed past Teresa into the hall. 'Don't bother coming back to the car with me. There's only a couple more bags.'

'I wasn't going to,' Teresa retorted, after her mother was safely out of the door. She left the shopping in its box, and ran upstairs, throwing herself down on her bed.

* * *

The letter was a single side of pale blue paper, sparingly covered in her father's small spiky handwriting. Teresa's eyes slid impatiently from 'My dear Teresa,' past the bits about the weather in Dublin and the trouble he was having with the software for his computer. Where was the bit about when he was coming over? He didn't mention that at all. The letter ended with something stupid about hoping she was working hard at school. As if he didn't know she always did!

She threw the letter down on the bed, then picked it up and re-read it more slowly. There was really nothing more to it than the weather and his work; it was polite, dutiful, like the letters Teresa wrote at Christmas and birthdays to the godmother she hardly knew. It gave Teresa a funny feeling to be reminded of them. There was a cheque inside the envelope; she hadn't looked at it. Now she picked it up and spread it flat. It was for twenty pounds. Again Teresa felt strange and embarrassed. It was too much, more than she wanted, and he hadn't sent Helen anything.

She threw both the letter and the cheque on the floor and lay back on her bed, trying to think. The noise of voices in the living room downstairs had been going on for some time, and she was just starting to wonder irritably what was going on, when her mother called up from the bottom of the stairs.

'Come down, will you, Teresa? There's someone I'd like you to meet.'

'Oh, what now?' Teresa muttered, hauling herself off the bed. 'Who?' she shouted, as she walked along the landing to the top of the stairs.

A young Indian was standing in the hall, grinning up at her. 'Me, I think,' he said.

Teresa came downstairs slowly. She didn't smile back at the man, but turned to her mother for an explanation. Nicola was standing in the doorway to the living room with a glass in her hand.

'You're drinking beer,' Teresa said incredulously.

'Velsford brought it,' Nicola said. 'He's staying to lunch.'

'Really,' said Teresa coldly.

She let them go ahead of her into the living room, where Helen was standing by the table, clutching a fistful of cutlery. She looked wildly over-excited; as Velsford came over, she jabbed at the air in front of him with a table knife.

'Let's have a sword fight!'

'Easy now,' said Velsford, lifting his glass to safety.

'He rescued me,' Helen called across to Teresa. 'He rescued me from a thug in an amusement arcade.'

'Serves you right for being there,' Teresa said repressively. She wasn't in the mood for whatever it was that was going on. There were three unopened cans of beer on the table. Was her mother planning to drink *more*?

'I had some of Velsford's beer,' said Helen, making a face. 'It was *disgusting*.' Seeing her mother take so easily to Velsford, Helen had let her own caution go. She was almost giddy with liking him by now.

'Helen,' her mother said warningly, 'that's enough. You go and sit down quietly for a few minutes or I'll have to send you upstairs.'

As Helen flung herself crossly into an armchair, Teresa went over to the piano and started playing a piece from memory. She was not sure whether she was trying to show off or trying to shut the others out.

'Wow,' said Velsford as she hit a wrong note and stopped abruptly. 'I'm impressed. How long have you been playing?'

'About six years,' said Teresa, a little proudly, laying her hands in her lap.

'I can play too,' said Helen forlornly from her armchair.

'For my age, I'm just as good as Teresa.'

'No, you're not,' said Teresa scornfully. 'Anyway, I thought you were giving it up.'

'God, you mustn't do that,' Velsford said, turning to Helen. 'It's a fantastic thing, to be able to play an instrument. I wish I'd had a chance to learn.' He leant over behind Teresa and dabbed at the keys softly with one finger.

Nicola looked at them with a smile. 'I'd better see to the lunch,' she said. 'I'll leave you two to keep Velsford amused. If there's any trouble, Velsford, just yell.'

She went into the kitchen, and started chopping vegetables.

Velsford smiled at Teresa. 'Play me something else,' he said. 'Do you know any jazz numbers?'

'No,' said Teresa in surprise. 'Well, I can do a bit of Scott Joplin, if that's any good.' She launched into *The Entertainer*, stumbling a bit here and there.

When she had finished, Velsford clapped. 'Excellent, I really mean it. Now, can I get you a drink?'

'No, thanks,' said Teresa primly.

'Are you sure? We got some diet Coke from the shop as well as the beer. Helen said you wouldn't drink the ordinary kind.'

Helen was getting restless with all the attention being paid to Teresa. 'Teresa's afraid of getting fat,' she said maliciously. 'It doesn't stop her eating Mars bars, though. Diet Coke and Mars bars, I ask you!'

Velsford smiled, but he obviously didn't think it as funny as Helen did. He turned back to Teresa, who hastily adjusted her face from the grimace she was directing towards her sister.

'Are you sure you won't have any Coke? I could put some ice and lemon in it. I'm good at fixing drinks. And then, maybe you can play us some more music.'

Teresa smiled, just slightly. 'Could I have a little bit of beer?' she asked. 'And then later I'll have a coke.'

Afterwards, Teresa thought they had never had a lunch like it. For one thing, Velsford wouldn't stay in his seat. He kept leaping up to help Nicola with plates, or fetch things from the kitchen, or to pick up Helen's napkin when she dropped it, which was every five minutes. Then there was the music. Velsford pleaded with Nicola to put a tape on while they were eating.

'It's good,' he insisted. 'It's relaxing. When you come and have a meal with me, I'll play you something really special. I hope you all like curry, by the way.'

'I think so,' said Nicola uncertainly, looking at the girls.

'I do,' said Teresa.

'And I do,' said Helen, not to be outdone.

Velsford beamed. 'Then I am going to make you the best curry you've ever tasted, and that's a promise.'

'Well, that's very kind of you,' Nicola began; but Velsford wouldn't let her continue.

'No way, no way! I'm not being kind. I'm just trying to welcome you into the neighbourhood, that's all, show you it's not all bike-stealing and money-snatching round here.'

'Or laughing at people in ballet clothes,' said Teresa.

'What?' Velsford was lost.

'Never mind,' said Teresa.

'Velsford,' Nicola said, 'if you don't start eating soon, your lunch will be cold.'

'Yes, of course, sorry.' He picked up his knife and fork, looked down at his plate and gave an embarrassed laugh. 'This looks great, but you haven't got any chilli sauce, have you? I really like that with stir-fry.'

They managed to keep him in his seat long enough for Teresa to fetch the Tabasco, and all three watched while he sprinkled it over the noodles and vegetables.

'You really like that?' Helen asked in a stunned voice.

Velsford grinned. 'I put chillies in everything.'

Helen giggled. 'What, even cornflakes?'

Teresa turned to her mother and rolled her eyes. Nicola decided she had better rescue the conversation.

'Well, you've told us you're a student, Velsford,' she said brightly, 'but you haven't said what exactly it is you study.'

'Not a lot,' Velsford said, and nudged Helen's foot under the table to make her laugh. Then he looked across at Nicola and his face went all guilty and nervous.

'Sorry, I shouldn't say that, should I? Not in front of your kids. It's just that, for me, there's so much happening in the world, life itself, if you get me. There are people to meet, ideas to talk about; life's not in a book, it's out there, it's happening –'

'What, in an amusement arcade?' Teresa said scornfully.

'Teresa,' said Nicola in a warning voice, but Velsford interrupted.

'No, she's right, she's totally correct. I wish I could be so – so straight.'

Teresa, meeting his eyes, wondered if he was making fun of her.

'Well, *I'm* glad you were in the amusement arcade,' Helen said, putting her arm through his.

'Music's stopped,' said Teresa, glad of the chance to get up from the table. 'What shall we have this time?'

'Something loud and cheerful,' Nicola said. 'Something to help me wash up.'

Velsford was on his feet immediately. 'I'll do it, I'll do it,' he insisted. 'You sit down, take it easy, have another beer.'

But he drank most of the beer himself in the end, drying the dishes while Teresa washed. Then Nicola made coffee and they sat down again at the table and drank it slowly, not saying very much. Velsford smoked a cigarette and hummed a little to the music. Helen brought out her origami books to impress him and then got absorbed, trying to make a whitte crane. When she got into difficulties with a particularly awkward fold, Velsford's deft fingers managed to rescue her.

Teresa tried to think about her father's letter, but found herself too full of lunch, too comfortable. She picked up a book, and half read, half watched Helen with Velsford. It was funny how nice it was having him around. When he finally left, at about five o'clock, Nicola went to the door with him and came back into the living room, laughing.

'Well,' she said. 'What on earth did you make of that?'

'I think he's lovely,' Helen said.

'We all know what you think,' Teresa said scathingly. 'You were practically sitting in his lap.'

Helen stuck out her tongue. 'Was not.'

'That's enough, you two, don't start an argument.' Nicola pushed back the hair from her forehead thoughtfully. 'I wonder if we should have said anything more definite about accepting his invitation.'

'I expect he'll phone or something,' Teresa said. 'If his curry's anything like the way he has his stir-fry, we won't be able to eat it anyway.'

'Wasn't he funny?' Nicola went over to the table and started picking up the coffee cups. 'We still don't know what he's studying.'

'I don't think it matters, does it?' Teresa said, with more than a trace of scorn. 'I mean, it doesn't seem to matter very much to *him*.'

'Well, he was very kind to Helen,' said Nicola, closing the argument in her own mind. 'Goodness, look at the time. The whole day's gone, and I've got such a headache from that beer. I'm not used to drinking during the day.'

'*What* did he say he was?' Teresa asked, coming back to Velsford.

'A Goan, darling, a Portugese Indian. Don't you remember that girl who was in your class at primary school? Gomes, or something like that, wasn't she called? Maria Gomes.'

'Oh, she was horrible,' Teresa said. 'I was glad when they moved. And did you see how many cigarettes he got through? Pretty disgusting.'

'You liked him, though, Teresa, so you might as well admit it,' Helen said yawning. She picked up the TV remote control and started flicking through the channels.

'At *least* switch off the music before you put on the television,' Nicola snapped. She went through into the kitchen and banged down the mugs in the sink. Teresa and Helen watched her go, then their glances met. With Velsford gone, all three were affected by the same sense of let-down. The afternoon had suddenly become flat and miserable.

'Mum said there was a letter from Dad,' Helen said, with her eyes back on the television. 'Did he say when he was coming?'

Teresa flung herself into a chair. 'No, he didn't,' she said crossly. 'He didn't say anything at all.'

Chapter Six

About two weeks later, Teresa sat on the school bus home, and watched her best friend Chrissie walk past her to sit with the boys from St Ignatius at the back. Chrissie had been going out with David Hutchinson for exactly eight days, and Teresa watched with hostility as he made room for her on the back seat. David wasn't exactly hideous or anything, just a bit thin and willowy with longish blond hair and too many spots. He and Chrissie were holding hands now, and whispering. Teresa wondered what they could find to talk about. David wore white towelling socks, his life's ambition was to meet Gazza, and he was in the bottom stream for everything except geography.

Two seats further up the bus, Karen Philips sat with Mike Moroney's arm clamped round her shoulders, a fixed smirk on her face as he leaned across her to talk to his mates. They were practically engaged, everyone said; and now Chrissie was at it too, meeting Dave outside the chip shop every lunch time, leaning against the wall and sharing a bag of chips with him where everyone would see. She was always with Dave now, every spare minute she had, and Teresa could never get a look in. Karen was the only girl Chrissie wanted to talk to any more, because Dave and Mike were best mates.

'Anyone sitting here?'

Teresa turned round, startled. It was Ann Carey, a thin girl with red hair and glasses, whom she didn't much like.

'No,' she said indifferently, and shifted her bag to make room.

Ann sat down, and lifted her own bag onto her knees. 'Masses of homework this weekend,' she said chattily. 'I haven't a clue about the maths, have you?'

Teresa let Ann ramble on about homework while her thoughts reverted gloomily to Chrissie. She wondered whether she would have gone out with David herself if he had asked her, which he never would. None of the boys from St Ignatius liked her much; they thought she was too clever. But if David had asked, she was depressed to realise, she would probably have said yes. She would be sitting in the back of the bus now, accepting the boredom and the dirty jokes as a fair swap for an arm round her shoulder. The point of a boyfriend wasn't what he was like. The point was having one.

As Teresa got off the bus, managing to shake off Ann Carey in the process, her mood was not improved by the fact that it had started to rain quite heavily. She began to walk at a smart pace towards home, her school bag dragging at her shoulder. It was only when she got to the corner of Arthur Street that she remembered what Nicola had said that morning; she was intending to pick up Helen from school and take her into town to buy some trainers. There would be no one at home to let her in.

Teresa felt inside her money belt for her keys and realised with a groan that she had left the whole bunch at school. She could visualise them, hanging from the keyhole of her metal locker, still there now for the cleaners to find. She had been closing the locker after getting out her P.E. kit to take home to wash, when Ann Carey (Ann again!) had come along and distracted her with a silly joke. What do you call a deer with no eyes? No idea, said Teresa indifferently, and Ann's face fell in disappointment. That was the answer, apparently. Ha-bloody-ha. It certainly wasn't worth getting locked out for.

She reached the house and peered up at the front bedroom window in case there was any chance of it being open. People climbed up the drainpipe, didn't they? But the window looked firmly closed, and Teresa didn't think she could get up the wet slippery drainpipe and wrest it open. The rain was still coming down and she was only in her blazer and summer uniform; she was going to get drenched. She rested her bag on the wall and began to swear.

After running through the words she could think of, and throwing in a few new combinations, she tried to think where she could go for shelter. There was the church not too far away, and the newsagent's even closer. They wouldn't mind her lurking, if she explained. She hoisted her wet bag onto her wet shoulder and turned to go, almost crashing into someone walking in the opposite direction, head down, hood up, and carrying two bags of shopping. When he swore, Teresa recognised the voice. It was Velsford.

'You didn't come round and have dinner,' he said, as she stooped to help him retrieve a carton of milk and a tin of tomatoes from the pavement. 'How come?'

'Well, you never phoned us,' Teresa replied defensively.

He looked funny in that dark green anorak, bundled up in his hood like a polar explorer. His glasses were misted over so she couldn't even see his eyes. She didn't tell him how she and Helen had searched the phone book in vain for a Fernandes. It made her feel silly and shy, meeting him now.

'You didn't need to fix a time,' he said. 'You could just have come round. How come you're out without a coat?'

Teresa laughed, and started to explain. Before she had properly finished, Velsford had taken her arm and was propelling her down the street.

'I get you, I get you,' he said. 'Now let's get you out of the rain. I don't want to have to explain to your mother that you got your pneumonia standing in the street being polite to me.'

'Hang on a minute,' Teresa said. 'Where are we going?'

'My place,' said Velsford. 'It's just around the corner.'

It wasn't much further than that. In a couple of minutes Velsford was fishing the key out of his pocket and opening the glass-panelled front door.

'In quickly,' he said, pushing Teresa forward while he organised his bags.

Teresa stepped in, wiping her feet vigorously on the mat. The house was similar in size and age to the one in Arthur Street, but it was less well cared for. The hall smelt faintly dingy, and the dark red carpet was covered in unidentifiable stains.

'Typical student house,' said Velsford defensively. 'And the living room's even worse.'

He opened the door for her. The sofa was covered in a dusty Indian cotton bedspread, as were the two sagging armchairs. There was a big cheese plant in one corner under a poster of a pink Cadillac. The only expensive-looking things in the room were the rented TV and video.

'It's nice,' said Teresa sincerely, brushing the wet strands of hair out of her eyes to look around. 'It must be great to have your own place.'

The dirty coffee cups and the litter of newspapers and magazines strewn across the sofa only added to its appeal. She would have hated to find a student house as clean and tidy as home.

'It would be great if the other two ever cleaned up after themselves,' said Velsford irritably, gesturing towards a dirty plate on the table. 'We're supposed to have a rota.'

Teresa was starting to notice the water dripping uncomfortably off her hair, onto her shoulders and down the back of her neck.

'You couldn't lend me a towel, could you?'

Velsford, who was pulling off his coat, jumped. 'God, yes, you're soaking. I'd better find something for you to change into. But a towel first. Wait, wait —' He let his coat drop onto the floor and darted out into the kitchen. He returned with a thin, fraying, blue towel.

'This is the only small one that's clean,' he said. 'Is it all right?' He looked so worried, Teresa wanted to laugh.

'It's fine,' she said. 'Here.' She took it from him and began to squeeze the dripping ends of her hair. Velsford watched her for a moment.

'That's not the way to do it,' he said. 'Will you let me?' He reached out for the towel and, draping it over her head, began to use it to pummel and massage her scalp and hair. Teresa let out a squeal of surprise.

'I'm not hurting you, am I?' Velsford lifted the towel and peered in.

'No, you're not, of course not,' Teresa giggled. 'It's just —'

'This is what my mum used to do if I was ever caught in the rain,' Velsford insisted. His small dark face with its expression of gentle concern, reminded Teresa of a mouse in a storybook; again she felt an impulse to laugh.

'No, you go ahead,' she said, and pulled the towel back down over her face.

Velsford began again, working on her scalp with strong fingers. Standing so close to him, feeling the touch of his hands, a strong pleasant pressure that made her scalp tingle, Teresa felt the desire to laugh at him suddenly leave her.

'There you are.' He pulled off the towel before she wanted him to finish. 'Now you won't get a cold, guaranteed.'

Teresa blew a wisp of hair away from her mouth, and

turned to face him. 'Thanks,' she said, feeling rather awkward.

Velsford suddenly reached up and pushed the hair gently back from her face. He was frowning as if the tenderness hurt him; when their eyes met, his were as startled and serious as her own.

'Clothes,' he said abruptly. He took her wrist and propelled her towards one of the chairs. 'You just sit there a minute, and I'll find you something to wear.'

When he came downstairs again, a sweater and a pair of jogging pants over his arm, Teresa jumped to her feet.

'Honestly, Velsford, I'm not that wet. I was wearing my blazer.'

'Look,' he said, pointing to the cotton cover of the chair, where Teresa had left a damp patch.

'Oh, sorry,' she said, and dabbed at it rather idiotically with her hand.

'It's not the chair I'm worried about,' Velsford said. 'Just change into something dry, all right? I'll give you a carrier for your clothes. Now let me show you where the bathroom is.'

Teresa followed him into the kitchen, where she caught a glimpse of plates and pans piled up in the sink, and bottles in a row on the worktop.

'Ignore the mess,' Velsford said. 'Chris had some people round last night and as usual went off this morning without clearing up. The bathroom's just through here.'

They went into a little hallway to the side of the kitchen, and Velsford swung open the bathroom door and put on the light.

'You should be able to find a big towel in the cupboard if you want one, but if not, give me a yell. I'll be in the kitchen, putting the kettle on.'

'Great,' said Teresa, and stepped inside. As she locked the bathroom door behind her, she could hear the tap running in the kitchen and the clatter of Velsford starting to wash up.

The bathroom was small and spartan, with white peeling paint and not a lot of room between basin, loo and bath. Teresa took off her blazer and hung it on the back of the door, then put down the loo seat and sat there to take off her sandals. She was wetter than she had realised. Her pink checked uniform dress was clinging to her legs and her skin was damp and chilled. She unbuttoned the dress and stepped out of it, then went, shivering, to the cupboard and pulled out the biggest towel she could see. She wrapped it round her, burying her chin in the rough peach folds until she felt warmth gradually spreading into her arms and legs. She stood for a while, feeling shy of putting on Velsford's clothes, shy of seeing him. When he knocked on the door a moment later, her heart banged violently, so that she couldn't hear what he was saying.

'Just coming,' she called through the door. She dressed hastily in the warm grey joggers and oversized sweater, then folded the towel and left it on the side of the bath. She picked up her own clothes and went through into the kitchen.

'Everything all right?' Velsford said. He was back at the sink, washing up. 'You seemed to be taking an awful long time.'

'Sorry,' Teresa said, surprised and a little offended. She looked round the kitchen. The stove was pretty disgusting, and all the surfaces needed a wipe, but there were lots of interesting packets and jars and a spicy mixture of smells. She pointed at a yellowing newspaper cutting, pinned up on one of the cupboards.

'Who's that?'

Velsford looked. 'Miles Davis. One of the greats.'

'Did you put it up? Do you like him?'

Velsford nodded. Something was making him uneasy,

Teresa realised. She took a surreptitious look down her front, but there were no buttons to be left undone. She began to roll up the sleeves of the sweater, trying to think of what to say next, when she heard a noise from the living room. Someone had put the television on. She turned to look, and saw a long-haired boy wearing jeans and a black t-shirt, lying stretched out on the sofa. He grinned at her and half raised a hand.

'That's Dave,' Velsford said in a low tight voice.

'Don't you like him?' Teresa whispered. That might explain it, she thought.

'No, he's fine, only of course he thinks –' To her relief, Velsford's face relaxed into a smile. 'Oh, never mind what he thinks. What would you like, tea or coffee? Or there's some of that instant hot chocolate stuff.'

'Hot chocolate,' said Teresa promptly.

She sat down at the small formica table and watched him make it, liking the shape of his head and the strong set of his neck and shoulders above his loose white shirt. When he brought the cups to the table he said, half-seriously, 'Your mum's going to think I've kidnapped you. She'll come round here with a big stick and beat me up.'

''Course not,' said Teresa. 'She likes you. She thinks you're really funny.'

Velsford pulled a face. 'I don't know if that's a compliment.'

'Well, I meant it as one,' Teresa said.

They drank for a little while in silence. Then Velsford said, 'Tell me something. Tell me what you want to do with your life. I know it's a big question, but give me an idea.'

'Oh, that's easy,' Teresa said eagerly. 'I either want to go to Cambridge to do English, or I want to go to music college. Or maybe, just maybe, I could be a ballet dancer, but I don't think that's very likely, because I've got a

66

problem with my Achilles tendon.'

As she spoke, Velsford broke into a smile that made Teresa redden and become embarrassed.

'Look, I didn't mean to show off,' she said. 'You asked me, that's all. If you want me to lie and pretend to be brainless, then you're as bad as the boys from St Ignatius.'

'Whoever they may be,' Velsford murmured. He looked at her with such obvious liking that Teresa was comforted.

'You're sensitive about being clever, aren't you?' he said. 'I wasn't laughing at you, I was impressed. Very impressed, in fact. I wish I'd been encouraged to do stuff like that, but Goans are too practical. They all want their kids to be doctors or accountants or engineers, things like that. That's why I'm doing this stupid business course. If I went home and told my mum I wanted to be an artist, she'd have a fit. How are you going to support a family on *that*, she'd want to know!'

Teresa smiled at him. 'It's funny to think of you having a mum.'

He looked at her in mock indignation. 'Why, where do you think I came from, under a mango tree?'

'No, I just meant —' Teresa didn't want to say it, it would sound so stupid. 'I just meant, I couldn't tell how old you are.'

'I'm twenty-one,' Velsford said.

'Seven years older than me,' said Teresa, looking at him.

'Seven years older than you,' Velsford echoed, and brushed her hand with his own.

'It's stopped raining,' Dave called, with a certain malice from the other room. Velsford looked over his shoulder at the kitchen window. 'He's right, it has.' He looked back at Teresa. 'Want me to walk over with you and wait till your mum gets back?'

'No, it's okay,' said Teresa reluctantly. 'I mean, it's gone five. She's probably back by now.'

'I'd better give her a ring then, and let her know where you are,' Velsford said, getting to his feet. 'Can you tell me the number?'

Teresa told him and heard him cross into the living room behind her and dial. She half hoped he would get no answer, but almost at once he was speaking, launching into explanations and laughter, and promises of coming round to see them all again soon.

'Bye,' he called, 'bye,' and, putting down the phone, he was back at her side. 'They've called off the search party,' he said with laughing eyes. 'Your mum trusts me, apparently.'

'It's me she trusts,' Teresa said smartly, then realised from the change in his face that it wasn't a clever thing to have said.

'Sorry, I only meant —'

'No, it's fine,' he said bleakly. 'Fine she trusts you, I mean. Have you got all your stuff?'

Teresa nodded towards her clothes, folded on the worktop. 'And I think my bag's in the hall,' she said.

'Good, let's go. I said I'd walk you to the corner.'

He insisted on carrying her school bag, so Teresa had only her clothes in a plastic carrier. They walked in silence, Teresa glancing once or twice at his closed face. She couldn't understand what she'd done to offend him so very much.

When they reached the corner, Velsford halted and said, still without meeting her eyes, 'Here we are. You'll be all right from here, won't you?'

'Of course I will,' Teresa said crossly. 'Where do you think we are, Bosnia or somewhere, with bombs whizzing round?'

'I'm just being careful,' he said doggedly. But when he handed over her bag, he couldn't avoid looking at her.

'Velsford . . .' she said. 'Honestly, I'm sorry. I was just

68

trying to be clever, and it wasn't.'

'You're telling me,' he said indignantly. Then he smiled. 'I'm sorry too, okay? I get a bit over-sensitive sometimes, especially with new people. It must be growing up in London that's done it. Someone's always trying to make fun at your expense there, if you're a wog.' He said it lightly enough, but Teresa winced.

'I'll see you soon,' he added, and punched her gently on the shoulder. 'Mean it.'

'Good,' said Teresa. She set off down the road, feeling too self-conscious to look back. She was sure he watched her until she got to the front gate.

Chapter Seven

Ten days later, Teresa and Helen were up in their bedroom. Both of them were supposed to be revising for the summer exams in two weeks, but Helen was taking one of her frequent breaks and lay on her bed, flicking through a comic. She had a slight cold and was breathing heavily through her mouth. Teresa was becoming increasingly irritated by that, and by all the other noises she kept making, rubbing her sandals against the side of the bed, coughing and rustling the pages of her comic. She wanted to put on some music, but Nicola had made her promise not to because it affected Helen's concentration. The irony of that made Teresa grimace.

'Teresa,' said Helen, throwing down her comic, 'if you had to choose between eating a bucket of worms or drowning a kitten, which would you choose?'

'Neither,' said Teresa shortly.

'No, but if you had to choose?'

'Christ, Helen!' Teresa shoved at her books irritably. 'It beats me where you get your drivel from.'

'It isn't drivel,' Helen said serenely. 'We were asking each other at school. Rachel Wilson said anyone who managed to eat school dinners would find a bucket of worms no problem.'

'Ho-ho, very droll. Now I've got a question for you.'

Helen sat up and looked alert.

'Why don't you just shut up and leave me alone?'

'All right,' Helen sighed, flopping back down on her bed. 'But I don't know how you can work. I'm too excited

70

wondering what this curry's going to be like.' She rolled over onto her stomach and looked at her sister shrewdly.

'You've been to his house. Are there loads of computers and books and stuff like that?'

'I've already told you,' Teresa said. 'I don't know why you keep asking.'

'Ah yes, but you didn't see his room, did you? He might be a secret genius.'

'Who, Velsford?' Teresa said in surprise. 'Somehow I doubt it.'

'Good, I'm glad of that,' Helen said.

'Why?' Teresa was ripe for an argument now. 'You mean you prefer people to be thick?'

'No, I mean I wouldn't like him to be like Dad,' Helen said. 'As it is, they couldn't be more opposite. Look at the way Velsford fixed up my bike for me on Saturday.'

'He only oiled it and pumped up the tyres,' Teresa said jealously.

'Yes, but he showed me how to do it,' Helen said. 'And he brought Mum that bottle of wine. I thought it was a bit rude of her not to open it. Velsford expected her to.'

Teresa turned round fully in her chair. 'Helen,' she said, 'people do not drink wine in the afternoon. Normal people don't, anyway.'

'Velsford wanted to,' Helen said. 'When we went outside to look at my bike he kept sort of hinting at it, but he wouldn't let me go inside and ask.'

'Don't talk rubbish,' said Teresa sharply.

'You weren't there,' Helen said. 'You were hanging round up here. You said you were busy, but when I came up here you weren't doing anything, just lying on your bed listening to some tacky music. That's twice Velsford's come round and you've been upstairs, so I don't know why you think you're such an expert on him.'

Teresa limited herself to a knowing smile.

Helen looked at her coolly. 'You know, the way you've been behaving, hanging round up here, then zooming down into the hall just as he was leaving, anyone would think you were in love with him or something.'

Teresa tittered, the way she did under pressure. 'Don't be so stupid, Helen. I'm not in love with anyone.'

'Good,' Helen said. 'He's miles too old for you, anyway.'

Teresa put on her most superior smile. 'Helen, when I need your advice about my love life, I'll just go and jump in a river or something, I'll be so desperate. Get the picture?'

Helen shrugged.

'And now I want to get some work done, thank you very much.' Teresa lowered her head over her books and pretended to be absorbed, but inside she was boiling with embarrassment. She had no idea Helen was so observant, the little rat.

For another quarter of an hour or so, there was silence between them, until their mother called up the stairs.

'Teresa! Helen! Time to get ready, both of you.'

Helen leapt off her bed and made for the door at once, but Teresa deliberately read to the end of the page she was revising before following her downstairs.

'There you are,' said her mother. 'I don't know why you can't come when you're called, Tess. We're supposed to be there in five minutes.'

Nicola had changed out of her trousers into a short pale yellow skirt and top. She was wearing her strappy shoes and amber beads and looked a little self-conscious.

'You didn't say you were going to dress up,' Teresa said suspiciously.

'I think she looks lovely,' Helen said.

Teresa ignored her. 'And you're wearing lipstick. *Mum —*'

'It's the first time we've been asked out since we moved here,' Nicola said rather defiantly. 'Besides, Velsford may have asked some other people, not just us. I don't see why I have to look like a bag lady just because my daughters expect it.'

'But I'm only in my jeans,' said Teresa. 'So's Helen.'

'In my shorts, actually,' Helen said, executing a clumsy pirouette. 'Not that I care.'

Nicola looked at her watch. 'There isn't time for you to change now. It's your own fault, Teresa, you should have come down the minute I called you.' As Teresa made an impatient gesture, she added quickly, 'Never mind, you're too young and pretty for what you wear to matter. You can have a squirt of my perfume, though, if you like.'

'Oh, don't be silly,' Teresa said ungraciously.

'I will, I will,' clamoured Helen, and insisted on spraying it on herself, with the result that the whole room stank of it by the time she had finished. She got in a squirt at Teresa, too.

'It's like all wearing the same dress,' Teresa complained as they set off. 'Besides, it's strong enough to kill flies.'

The other two ignored her. They talked about Velsford all the way down the street.

'Someone's playing music very loud,' Nicola said as they turned into Velsford's road. When they got to his house, they knew where it was coming from. The front door was open and music was blasting out into the street.

'That's African jazz,' said Helen authoritatively.

The other two looked at her.

'How on earth would you know?' Teresa demanded.

'That's what Velsford said he was going to play,' Helen replied smugly.

'Well, shall we go inside?' Nicola peered into the hall. 'There doesn't seem much point in knocking.'

Just then, Velsford appeared inside the house. He shouted something none of them could hear, and disappeared again. A moment later the music was reduced to background level. Velsford reappeared and came down the hall towards them. He was wearing a finely embroidered Indian muslin shirt and matching baggy white trousers. The shirt had a deep v-neck, so you could see part of his chest. Teresa felt suddenly embarrassed. In those clothes he didn't look like Velsford any more, but a stranger.

'Wow, you look lovely,' he said to Nicola, his voice full of pleased surprise.

'I'm glad I dressed up myself now. Another minute, and I'd have gone upstairs to change back into my jeans.'

Teresa burst out, 'I was going to dress up too, but Mum said there wasn't time.'

Both her mother and Velsford looked at her in that kind adult way; she wanted to bite her tongue out, it made her feel so stupid. Then Velsford yelled, 'Helen! What are you doing hiding behind your mum? You've got to come and help me in the kitchen.'

'You want Helen to help you?' Nicola said incredulously.

'I promised,' Helen said. 'We made a deal last Saturday. If Velsford helped me with my bike, I had to help him make a — what was it?' She turned to Velsford, her face perplexed.

'A raita,' he said grinning. 'You're going to make the raita yourself, and you're going to help me make a vegetable curry.'

Helen smiled blissfully.

'I'm going to have to borrow you, Velsford,' Nicola said. 'I can never get her to do anything at home.'

'She's too lazy to do anything, even her homework,' Teresa said spitefully.

'Now that I can relate to,' Velsford said. 'I've got an essay waiting upstairs I should have handed in the week before last.'

'Velsford!' Nicola exclaimed reproachfully. 'You shouldn't have invited us if you were busy. It would have kept till another time.'

Velsford waved that away. 'I'd rather have company than work,' he said. 'Come inside.'

They followed him into the living room, which had been tidied up since Teresa's visit. The newspapers and coffee cups had gone, and there was a white cloth on the table. On the sideboard was a vase of yellow flowers, and the covers of the sofa and chairs had all been smoothed down.

'Dave isn't here, then?' Teresa asked as she looked round.

'They both might be back later,' Velsford said. 'Now, who'd like a drink?'

Nicola started fishing in the carrier bag she had brought with her. 'For you,' she said, bringing out a bottle of red wine.

Velsford's face lit up. 'Thanks,' he said. 'Thanks very much. Let's start with this one, then.' He went out and came back with glasses and a corkscrew and opened the bottle with practised efficiency.

'I'll have some too, please,' said Teresa rather aggressively, as Velsford gave Nicola the first glass.

Velsford looked round at Helen. 'And what about the chef's assistant?'

'I don't think so,' said Nicola firmly. 'Not if you're hoping to get any work out of her.'

'Okay,' said Velsford, taking a swallow out of his own, rather brimming, glass. 'Helen sticks to Coke. Shall we get started on the cooking, then?'

'We can come and watch, can't we?' Teresa said, taking

a step after them. But Nicola touched her arm, just perceptibly shaking her head.

'You two get on with it,' she said to Velsford. 'Teresa and I will put on some music and relax, won't we?'

'Why?' Teresa demanded in an angry undertone.

'Because Helen will be more comfortable that way,' her mother said, and moved across the room to look at a poster.

Teresa lingered at the record player for a long time, so she could watch Velsford and Helen through the open kitchen door. But eventually, under the pointed stare of her mother, she went over to the sofa and sat down with a bad grace. She sipped her wine and thought how stupid it was to be left with only her mother to talk to.

'They can't be very comfortable here in winter,' Nicola observed. 'That gas fire's tiny, and they don't seem to have central heating.'

Teresa didn't bother to reply. Then her mother saw the pot plants and started to exclaim about their condition.

'Do you suppose those African violets are Velsford's? I wonder how he looks after them. Mine always die.'

Teresa yawned. She wished she liked red wine better; at least if she got drunk, she wouldn't be wasting the entire evening.

'To think I'm missing *Top of the Pops* for this,' she said aloud.

Her mother looked at her in surprise. 'I'm sorry, darling, I thought you wanted to come.'

'Of course I did,' Teresa said. She sighed impatiently. 'It's just —'

'Just what?'

'Oh, never mind.'

Nicola looked at her with raised eyebrows, but did not pursue the subject. She went over to the record player, picked up the sleeve of the record they were listening to, and sat down to read the notes on the back. Teresa looked out of the window into the street. A few minutes later Helen came back in, carrying something in a bowl which she set down carefully on the table.

'Goodness, darling, that looks lovely,' Nicola said.

'That's the raita,' Helen said in a pleased voice. 'Velsford told me what to do, but I did it all myself.'

'Huh, it's only yoghurt,' Teresa said, coming over to peer at it.

'And spices,' Helen said indignantly. 'Roasted and ground spices on the top, look. And I had to peel and slice the cucumber.'

'Well, I'm definitely coming to watch you make this curry,' Teresa said with a cynical grin.

'No, you are not,' Helen retorted.

'For goodness' sake —' Nicola began, then caught Velsford's eyes as he came out of the kitchen, and laughed in embarrassment. 'They're not always like this, honestly!'

'Teresa is,' said Helen. 'Teresa's horrible.'

In the end, everyone went into the kitchen. Nicola sat at the table chatting to Velsford while Helen cut up onions and green beans and chopped garlic under his direction. Teresa stood in the doorway, feeling out of things. Helen wouldn't let her do anything to help, and Nicola insisted it was up to Helen to decide. Teresa sipped her wine, watching Velsford as he tried to cook, answer the stupid questions their mother kept asking, and prevent Helen from cutting herself, all at the same time.

'So did your parents meet before they came to this country, or afterwards?'

'Afterwards,' said Velsford, bending over Helen to correct the way she was holding the knife. 'You'll chop your fingers off if you do it like that,' he said.

'And your mother's family came from Pakistan?'

'Yes, when she was about fourteen or fifteen. She and

my dad met in London. They live in Edmonton now.'

'Is that a nice bit?' Nicola asked. 'I don't know London very well.'

Velsford grinned. 'It shows,' he said.

'And do you have any brothers and sisters?' Nicola persisted. She caught sight of Teresa's disapproving face and started to laugh. 'Sorry,' she said. 'This is turning into an interrogation, but really we know hardly anything about you, and you know all about us.'

'He doesn't know about Dad,' Helen said.

Velsford turned from the pan of onions browning on the stove and looked at Nicola enquiringly.

'He writes detective stories,' she explained. 'Sort of religious thrillers. You might have heard of him — who knows, you might even be a fan.'

Velsford looked uncertain. 'It's not my favourite sort of reading. What name does he write under?'

'Stephen Flynn,' Teresa said. 'His books are all set in Ireland. His detective's a priest called Monsignor Septimus Pym.'

'Sorry,' Velsford gave an apologetic shrug.

'I knew you wouldn't have heard of him,' Helen said gleefully.

Teresa couldn't let her get away with that. 'There's no reason why he should,' she said rather coldly. 'It's not as if they're best sellers or anything. A lot of reviewers seem to think they're too clever ever to be really popular.'

'A bit like your father, in fact,' Nicola murmured, draining her wine glass. Teresa stared at her reproachfully, but didn't know what to say in front of Velsford. He looked round again.

'You're not together then, you and —' He seemed uncertain how to finish the sentence.

'No, we're not, no,' said Nicola. 'We separated fairly recently. I'm afraid it hit Teresa rather hard.' She smiled

78

across at her daughter, who winced in embarrassment.

'Oh, I see,' Velsford said. He went on stirring the onions in silence.

Just as it was starting to get uncomfortable, he nudged Helen on the shoulder. 'Wake up, partner, it's time to put in all those spices I got you to grind.' He made her take over the stirring, and only helped her by telling her when it was time to add things. When the curry was ready, he tasted it, and held out the spoon for Helen to try.

'Excellent, really excellent,' he said. 'Are you sure there isn't some Goan blood in your family somewhere along the line?'

'Don't be silly!' Helen blushed with pleasure. 'I only cut things up. You told me how to do everything else.'

'No way!' Velsford looked across at Nicola and grinned. 'I think this girl knows how to cook. I think at home she's only pretending she can't do it.'

'Oh, I'm sure of that,' Nicola said dryly.

'Now there's one last decision we have to make,' Velsford said, looking round for his glass. 'Do we want rice or chapattis?'

Helen and Teresa looked at each other warily.

'We've never had chapattis,' Teresa said.

'Really?' Velsford was surprised. 'Home-made ones are very good. They're easy to make, too. But we can have rice if you'd rather.'

'Couldn't we have both?' Nicola suggested. 'Or is that like having chips with mashed potato?'

Velsford shook his head and grinned. 'Both is fine. Let's clear a bit of space, and we can get going.'

Helen, under pressure from both Velsford and her mother, was brought to agree that it was only fair to let Teresa join in making the chapattis. A production line was quickly established, with Velsford rolling out the dough, Nicola cooking the chapattis in a flat pan and the two girls finishing them over a hot flame. That part could be quite spectacular; when Velsford showed them how to do it, the chapatti puffed up like a little cushion as the hot air filled it, and it seemed a pity to have to put it on a plate to get flat again. Teresa reckoned that it was her turn now for praise, but Helen kept all the luck. Time and again her chapattis rose, golden and full, while Teresa's struggled to lift a corner or remained stubbornly flat.

'Don't worry, the taste is just as good,' Velsford said, giving her arm a reassuring squeeze, but Helen's self-satisfaction was almost more than Teresa could bear.

Everything was ready at last, and when they carried the dishes through to the living room table, Teresa was surprised to realise how hungry she was. Velsford leapt up to refill glasses and change the music.

'Start, start,' he urged Nicola. 'Help yourself to everything.'

'I'm not quite sure how we should eat this,' Nicola admitted.

Velsford filled his own plate, and demonstrated. 'You can mix the rice in with the curry and eat it with your fingers, if you want,' he said. 'That's how my mum eats at home. And with the chapattis, you just break a bit off and use it as a scoop. No forks needed, really.'

'Sounds messy,' said Helen happily.

'Don't put ideas into her head,' Nicola said. 'She'll try it at home, and I'll never get the stains out of the tablecloth.'

Teresa was looking at her plate with a slightly sinking feeling. The vegetables and the rice looked all right, but the meat wasn't at all familiar. It was in big chunks, still on the bone, and there were strange twig-like bits in it, as though the sauce had been dropped on a forest floor and scraped back into the pan.

'What are these bits, Velsford?' she asked gingerly.

'Spices,' he said in surprise. 'You know, cinnamon, cardamon, stuff like that. Chillies, too, of course. Just push them to the side of your plate, they're not meant to be eaten.' He picked up a chunk of meat between his fingers, and started to eat.

Nicola, with a slightly embarrassed laugh, said, 'Well, I'm sorry, Velsford, but I'm going to stick to my fork. You two girls can do what you like, of course.'

Helen pulled off a piece of chapatti, and dabbed it in her plate enthusiastically. Teresa, with slight reluctance, wrapped a piece of chapatti round some meat and put it in her mouth.

'It's good!' she said in distinct surprise.

'Very good,' Helen echoed.

Velsford was happy. 'You helped to make it,' he said.

There was no pudding, to the mild surprise and disappointment of the visitors. After the plates were cleared, the kettle was put on for coffee, and Velsford brought it in, looking round him with satisfaction.

'This is almost like being at home,' he said. 'It's nice to spend time with a family.'

Teresa threw him a challenging glance. 'Don't you like living here, then?'

He met her gaze with a slightly quizzical grin. 'Of course I do. And the thing I like about your family is that it isn't my family, do you get me?'

Teresa wasn't at all sure that she did, but there was no time to say anything before he had moved on to something else. He pulled out his cigarettes and looked across at Nicola rather guiltily.

'Do you mind?'

'Don't be silly, it's your house,' she said briskly. 'And you needn't worry about tempting these two. They're much more likely to bother you into giving them up than to succumb to your evil influence.'

'You can say that again,' Helen chipped in. 'Smoking's dis-*gusting*.'

Teresa was starting to get restless. It was no good trying to have any serious sort of conversation with Velsford with the others present; they took up too much of his attention. And in spite of that business about families being nice, she couldn't really believe he was doing it out of anything more than politeness. Well, maybe some people might find Helen cute and interesting; the problem was, when they did, Helen knew it, and played up to it. She'd really hogged his attention tonight, all right. And even now, they were talking about things to do with Helen, her problems at school and stuff.

'Hey, listen!' Velsford's concerned expression suddenly lit up. 'Do you mind if I turn this up?'

'The Beatles,' said Helen with pleasure, and began to sing quietly along with the tune.

Nicola laughed. 'I remember all of these from the first time round,' she said. 'I never dreamt then that I'd be listening to my own daughter singing them.'

'"Let's all get up and dance to a song that was a hit before your mother was born"' Velsford quoted, smiling at her.

'Well, almost,' said Nicola. 'Oh, they were amazing, weren't they? Good days for me, too.'

And when the song was over, she began to tell Velsford about her own student days, the time before Stephen Flynn and babies, when she climbed onto the college roof with a banner, and hitch-hiked down to London to protest outside the American embassy. This was all new to Teresa, and she listened with a kind of jealous surprise, watching Velsford's absorbed face with resentment.

As the stories continued, something very strange happened, which caused Teresa a moment of pure panic. For a brief time, her mother was no longer her mother, but a stranger, a *person*, with an unknown history, unknown possibilities. That was how others saw her. Perhaps that was how Velsford saw her. Teresa's jealousy mounted; she was a child in an adult's game, and nothing she could offer could compete with this glamour, this superior attraction. The spell was broken by Helen's voice.

'Wow, Mum, I didn't know you'd done all that,' she said in simple admiration.

'Oh, it was a long time ago,' Nicola said. She smiled ruefully. 'I've changed a lot since then.'

'Nonsense,' said Velsford. His voice was warm and admiring. 'I wish the girls I know at the university had half your spark.'

Nicola seemed a little embarrassed now. She glanced at her watch, and exclaimed, 'Goodness, look at the time! We must go, girls. School tomorrow.'

'Oh, *Mum* –' Helen protested.

Teresa, still shaken, was anxious to get away. 'Come on, Lennie,' she said, getting to her feet. 'Don't make a fuss.'

Nicola was groping under the table for her bag. When she found it, she straightened up, and smiled at Velsford.

'Well, thank you,' she said. 'I haven't had such a nice evening for a very long time.'

He nodded. He too was on his feet now, and he moved away from the table towards Nicola. He wore a worried, slightly guilty look.

'You being on your own and everything,' he said. 'You know, if you ever feel like going to see a film or something, and you've got no one to go with –'

Nicola hesitated a fraction. 'Thank you, Velsford,' she said. 'That's very kind.'

A huge wave of relief washed through Teresa, who had been watching and listening intently to all of this. Velsford was only being kind! She couldn't have stood it otherwise, but that 'kind' made everything clear. She looked affectionately towards her mother.

'It's been a brilliant evening,' she said.

'Yes, and now all we've got to look forward to are the exams, and then Dad coming,' Helen said dolefully, trailing towards the door.

'You're over-tired,' said her mother, putting an arm around her.

Velsford came out with them into the hall. He punched Helen lightly on the shoulder. 'See you soon, Miss. Thanks for cooking dinner.' When he turned to Teresa, she was confused to see the quizzical look back in his eyes.

'No hiding upstairs next time I come round, all right?'

Teresa didn't know what to say; she searched his face for a clue to his meaning, but he didn't stay still long enough. He was clowning with Helen's baseball cap, and waving them out of the door. He stood in the doorway, looking out after them, until they turned the corner and the house was out of sight.

'Nice,' said Nicola, yawning.

'Very nice,' agreed Helen, swinging her arm through her mother's. But Teresa said nothing at all.

Chapter Eight

It was the second time in a week that Nicola was going out for the evening. While she was getting ready, Helen trailed into her bedroom, looking miserable.

'What's the matter?' Nicola asked, hauling furiously at her tights. 'Can't Teresa help? I'm in an awful rush.'

They executed a sort of dancing manoeuvre, Nicola moving towards the mirror, and Helen sliding round her to the bed, where she pulled discontentedly at the rejected outfits laid out on the duvet.

'Do you have to go out tonight?' she demanded.

'What's the matter, aren't you feeling well?' Irritation struggled with concern in her mother's expression. 'Come here and let me feel your forehead.'

'It's not exactly that I don't feel well,' Helen said, taking comfort from the cool firmness of her mother's hand and hoping she might be discovered to have a raging fever.

'Well, what is it, then?' Nicola demanded, letting her hand drop rather impatiently. 'You haven't got the slightest temperature, that's for sure.'

'It's just —'

'Just what?' As she spoke, Nicola continued to get ready. She reached for her earrings and clipped them on. 'I think I'll leave my hair down. It looks better, don't you think?'

Helen nodded reluctantly. 'You never used to go out when Dad was at home,' she said.

'I never liked to leave you with him,' Nicola replied. She

took both Helen's hands and looked attentively at her troubled face. 'Come on, what's really the matter? Don't you like being left with Teresa? You didn't make this fuss on Tuesday when I went to see that film with Velsford.'

'I didn't mind you going with Velsford,' Helen said. 'It's just tonight. I don't know who you're going with.' She willed her mother to understand, staring at her unhappily. 'I don't mind if it's Velsford,' she repeated.

'Listen to me,' Nicola said kindly. 'I'm only going to a restaurant with a gang of teachers from the school. I told you all about it, didn't I? It's just a get-together, to celebrate the end of term. You know Caroline, and Ann, so you do know who I'm going with. It's Ann's car I'm going in, and we're bound to be back early because we've all got children and it's school tomorrow. I expect I'll be at home by ten-thirty at the latest. And you'll be safe here with Teresa in charge. I'll tell her to let you go to bed a bit later than usual.'

'I bet she won't,' Helen said sulkily, only partly reassured.

'I'll have a word with her,' Nicola said. 'No, Ann'll be here any minute to pick me up. Can you find my shoes under the bed?'

'Which, these?' Helen said, fishing up a dirty trainer.

'Oh, Helen, don't be so childish,' Nicola said, half amused, half exasperated. 'Go down and tell Teresa I want to speak to her, will you?'

When Teresa showed a sullen face round the bedroom door, it was suddenly too much.

'Don't you two realise I'm entitled to some life of my own?' Nicola exploded. 'You're making me feel like a criminal. Dear God, do other mothers have to go through all of this?'

Teresa shrugged indifferently. 'I wouldn't know,' she said. 'And I'm not planning on finding out by personal experience. There are too many people in the world as it is.'

'Well, unfortunately, it's too late for me to do anything about my contribution to the population explosion,' Nicola said dryly. 'All I wanted to tell you, Tess, was that I shouldn't be back much later than ten-thirty. Helen's feeling vulnerable, so go easy on her, all right? No persecution about school work, and if she wants to stay up a bit later than usual, she has my permission.'

'Okay,' Teresa said reluctantly.

'That goes for you, too. Have you got a lot to do?'

Teresa shook her head. 'They don't give us anything in the last week of term, except finishing-up projects, and I've done all mine.'

'Well, why don't you play Cluedo or something with Helen?' Nicola suggested. 'You haven't done that for ages. Oh God, was that a car hooting? I must find my shoes!'

'Mum says we have to play Cluedo,' Teresa announced grimly when she went downstairs. They didn't, of course. They watched a comedy on ITV that they weren't normally allowed to watch, and when it was over Teresa said cheerfully, 'Come on, Lennie, let's have a look at your maths stuff.'

Helen ignored her, staring at the television in stubborn silence.

Teresa didn't know whether to laugh or get annoyed. She said, 'Look, you promised Mum you'd do some every day after your exam results were so abysmal.'

Helen turned her head. 'With her, not you. Anyway, she said starting in the holidays.'

'Please yourself.' Teresa shrugged. 'You can do what you like, then, but we're not watching this rubbish. There's something else I want to see.'

This turned out to be a foreign film that Teresa was sure must be about sex, although all the characters seemed to do

87

was talk about the meaning of life and go for long walks in the forest.

'This is boring,' Helen complained after half an hour. 'You might as well put on the news. At least it's in English.'

But Teresa kept tight hold of the remote control, so Helen went into the kitchen and spent a long time constructing a mammoth sandwich. When she came back, she found Teresa had changed channels and was watching a repeat of an Agatha Christie serial. As soon as it finished, Teresa tried to send her to bed. Helen refused to go unless they both went, and Teresa was forced in the end to give in, since it went against the grain to have Helen still up when her mother came in, no matter her mother's views on the subject.

They lay in the dark, neither talking, both aware that the other was still awake. Helen lay curled up and rigid, fists sandwiched between her knees, listening for the sound of a car pulling up outside. She had got through the evening, but this was the difficult bit, when Teresa's company did not help. What if Mum should be late? What if she never came back, but died in a car crash? It was all right when she went out with Velsford; nothing bad could happen then. But this wasn't Velsford, this was strangers. And if anything happened to Mum, Dad would be in charge. Teresa had made that quite clear.

Teresa was also thinking about her father. She lay with her eyes open, staring up at the ceiling through the dusky light. Dad was coming in two weeks, according to his last letter. He would be staying in the old house, alone, and taking them on visits. It was all so strange, Teresa didn't know how to think about it. It was like the way she had felt when, a few weeks ago, she had gone back to look at the old house. She had gone there after school, walking back from the school bus stop with her bag banging

88

against her shoulder, down the familiar street up to the gate. The house looked just the same, except for the empty windows and the long grass. Every inch of the place was familiar. Teresa had opened the gate and walked up to the front door. Everything was familiar, but the meaning was missing. It wasn't her house any more.

A faint noise from the other bed brought her back to the present.

'What's the matter, Lennie?' she called out.

'Nothing,' Helen said in a small voice. 'I just can't get to sleep.'

'Why's that?' Teresa asked sympathetically. 'Worried about school?'

'No, it's just Mum's out so late,' Helen said. 'It gets on my nerves.'

'I told you what it would be like.' Teresa sat up. 'Nights out with the girls, women's meetings — this is just the beginning, Lennie old girl.'

'Well, I don't like it,' Helen said fretfully. 'Why can't she just go out with Velsford?'

That took the smile off Teresa's face. She kicked the duvet restlessly. 'Why can't we all go, you mean,' she said. 'That last film they went to see was only a fifteen. They could have let me come quite easily.'

'Teresa, you aren't half thick sometimes,' Helen said.

'What do you mean?' Teresa peered at her suspiciously through the dark.

Helen wedged herself up on one elbow. 'Well, what do you think I mean? They'd take us if they wanted to, that's pretty obvious. So they must want to go on their own. Now do you get it?'

Teresa felt her face redden. She spoke in a quick angry voice. 'I suppose you think you're being really clever, don't you? Well, you're miles out, brainbox. Velsford's only being kind to Mum. She said so herself. Anyway, she's twice his age, and she's — she's *Mum*, for God's sake. It's ridiculous to think of her going out with anyone. And you'd better keep your mouth shut, all right, and not go round saying stupid things like that, or —'

'Or what?' Helen said coldly. 'It isn't stupid, and it wasn't even my idea in the first place. It was Katie and Miles, that time when Velsford came to church with us. they thought he was great. Anyway, I wouldn't mind. I think it would be brill if he and Mum got together.'

Teresa didn't answer. She started to get out of bed.

'Where are you going?' Helen asked a little anxiously.

'Downstairs,' Teresa said from the door. 'I'm not staying up here if you're going to talk rubbish.'

Helen heard the angry bump of Teresa's bare feet on the stairs and, a moment later, the sound of the television from the living room. She lay back and waited. Twenty minutes later came the noise of a car pulling up outside the house. A woman's voice called goodnight, the car door slammed and then her mother's key was in the lock. Helen turned on her side contentedly and went to sleep. Downstairs, Teresa got out of her chair and faced the door, rigid with anger. As her mother came in, she turned a blazing face on her. Nicola, bending to ease off first one shoe, then the other, barely glanced in her daughter's direction.

'Everything all right, Tess? I take it Helen is in bed. Lovely Italian restaurant Caroline found for us. You mustn't tell Helen, but I succumbed to temptation and had the veal.' She looked up then.

'What's the matter?' she said in alarm. 'Teresa, what's happened?'

Teresa had to clear her throat to speak. 'You can go out with whoever you like,' she said in a high, barely controlled voice. 'Friends, men even — I don't care, it's not my business. But if you ever bring someone home, if it ever gets to be serious, then I'm walking out of here. No way am I going to put up with a stepfather. Dad's who you're married to, remember?'

Before her mother had time to take it in, before she had time to speak, Teresa was out of the room and running, back upstairs to bed. She was banking on the fact her mother would not follow her, would not risk waking Helen and upsetting her with a scene. Teresa got into bed and sat upright, hugging her knees and listening intently. Nothing. Her mother had stayed downstairs.

When her father came she would tell him something; she wasn't sure what yet, but something. This was no good, this couldn't go on. She felt afraid and somehow guilty; ashamed, almost, of thinking of her mother in that way, and desperately disappointed about Velsford. Surely it couldn't be true, what Helen had said? But if it was, Teresa felt that it was, in some obscure way, her fault. She had done the damage by not thinking enough about her father, by letting the old house go. Dad had been out of her thoughts for a while, and she had been almost reluctant to write to him. No wonder the others had forgotten about him too.

She lay down and tried to summon back the fantasy she had invented when they first moved to Arthur Street, the picture through which she had drifted into sleep. Dad was standing in the hallway of the old house, one arm around Helen and the other around Mum, looking across at Teresa with love and gratitude. Somehow (the dream was always hazy about the details) she had solved the crisis, brought her family back together, worked a happy ending. The picture stayed steady for only a moment, then dissolved into unease. Guiltily, greedily, Teresa turned to another horde of images, and fell asleep as Velsford reached forward to touch her cheek.

Teresa woke next morning with a sense of something resolved, a feeling of calm and contentment that lasted until she heard her mother's voice, cold and tired, calling them from the bottom of the stairs. Teresa pulled the duvet over her head and lay for a few minutes, thinking of nothing, then got up and went downstairs. Her mother was sitting waiting at the table, red-eyed and angry.

'I don't know what got into you last night,' she said coldly, 'but I want an explanation.'

'What? What?' demanded Helen, coming in after Teresa in her pyjamas. 'What did she do?'

'Nothing that's any concern of yours,' Nicola said sharply. 'Teresa, I'm waiting.'

Helen slid into her place at the table and shook cereal into her bowl, looking from Teresa to her mother expectantly. Teresa walked past them both into the kitchen and switched the kettle on. She stood waiting for it to boil and wished them all away — mother, father, Velsford, Helen. Life was too much. Life was on the black rocks, with no rescue in sight.

'Teresa, I'm still waiting,' her mother called from the other room. 'I'm not letting you leave this house until I've had an explanation and an apology.'

Teresa bit her lip. She went back into the living room.

'Forget it,' she said with an uncomfortable little laugh. 'Forget I ever said it, okay? It was stupid. I know you'd never do anything like that.'

'Teresa!' Her mother sounded so angry, Teresa flinched. She waited as Nicola got to her feet and came round the table to confront her.

'What are we talking about here?' her mother demanded, forcing Teresa to keep her eyes on her angry face. 'My right to choose who I spend time with? My right to be a normal adult with normal friendships? Am I to do without' them just because I've got an over-sensitive teenage daughter?'

'So you mean you are going out with someone, then?'

Teresa kept up a smile, but her heart was pounding in her chest.

'I mean it's none of your business whether I am or not!' Nicola stared at her, eyes blazing. 'I will not have my children running my life, Teresa. I do not belong to you and Helen, not exclusively. There's a part of me that belongs only to myself. Your father did his best to destroy it, and I'm not letting you finish the job.'

Teresa was out of her depth now. She wasn't even sure they were still talking about the same thing. Why couldn't her mother just give a straight answer, instead of getting into this — this human rights rubbish? Shaken, she took refuge in sarcasm.

'And I thought you were such a good Catholic,' she said pityingly. 'All that church on Sundays. All those vows you made to Dad.'

Nicola pushed back her hair from her forehead with a wild gesture. She was so angry she hardly knew how to express it. As she opened her mouth to shout, Helen chipped in eagerly, 'Is there someone else, Mum? Is it Velsford?'

Disconcerted, Nicola swung round. 'So you're at it too, are you? Two trips to the cinema, and you've got me divorced and remarried!'

'Why not?' Helen said. 'I think it would be very nice.'

'Oh, do you?' Nicola looked at her, not knowing whether to be maddened or amused. 'The point is, though, Lennie, I'm not asking what you think.'

She turned to appeal to Teresa, too, speaking more calmly now. Teresa had time to think how unfair it was that Helen could get away with saying anything, while she always got blamed.

'Look,' Nicola said. 'You know when there's any major decision to be made I consult you and take your feelings into account. You know that, both of you. So I'm simply not having you breathing down my neck every time I spend a few hours out of the house in adult company.' She raised a hand as Teresa attempted to speak. 'No, Teresa, I'm not discussing it. I'm entitled to my own life, and time to spend with the first new friend I've had for years.' The edge came back into her voice as she added, 'And I don't need reminding of my marriage vows by you, thank you very much.'

'Sorry,' said Teresa in a subdued voice, and moved towards the kitchen.

She was only partly reassured. If Velsford was simply Nicola's friend, why didn't she just say so plainly? Why wouldn't she say outright there was nothing more to it than Velsford's kindness? As she put on the kettle again, and fetched a mug, she couldn't help wondering if Velsford was seeing her mother just as a way of getting friendly with all of them, with her. She permitted herself a small smile. Next time she went round to his house, she would shake off Helen somehow, and see what happened.

Behind her in the living room, Nicola sat down again, picked up her coffee cup and drank down the cold remains. Helen began to crunch cereal. After a minute, she risked a brief smile at her mother. Nicola smiled back, a little reluctantly, and Helen relaxed. Things were getting back to normal. As the sound of Teresa making coffee came through from the kitchen, Nicola called through to her in her normal voice, 'I'd love another cup, if you're making some.'

Teresa came in, and took her mother's mug without looking at her. But when she returned with the coffee, Nicola grasped her wrist as she put the mug down on the table.

'I'm almost afraid to mention this after all the uproar there's been, but Velsford's coming round this evening. Do you remember we said we would paint the hall in the summer holidays? Well, he's offered to help. I thought we could go to that big DIY superstore tonight and choose the paint. Would either of you two like to come?'

'I would,' Helen said promptly.

Teresa hesitated. 'All right,' she said, trying to keep the disappointment out of her voice. It looked like she would never get Velsford on his own.

They finished up in the café, cokes and giant cookies all round, after forty minutes hard negotiating up and down the immense aisles stacked with tins of paint and rolls of wallpaper. Helen had wanted an impossible shade of pink emulsion, but settled at last for the compromise apricot.

'It'll make the hall look even smaller than it is,' Teresa warned, wishing she had held out for simple white.

'It's a nice warm colour,' her mother said. 'You'll appreciate it next winter.'

'Don't even mention next winter,' Velsford said with a shiver. 'It must be in the blood or something, but I can't stand the winters here. I don't want to have to think about it for at least another six months.'

'When are we going to start painting?' Helen asked, sucking noisily on her straw.

'Whenever you like,' Velsford looked towards Nicola. 'It's very nice of you to give me the job. My overdraft was starting to give me nightmares.'

Teresa stared. 'Is Mum paying you? I didn't know.'

'Of course I'm paying Velsford for his time,' Nicola said, with a swift apologetic glance at Velsford. 'It's a very big job. The old paper has to be stripped off and replaced before he can even start painting. I don't like to think how much a decorator would charge us.'

'Well, I'm just glad I can put off going home,' Velsford said. 'I hate having to live off my mum in the holidays, and there's no work for students anywhere at the moment.

Who wants to take someone on for just a few weeks? I'll be off to France soon for the grape-picking, and then I'll have to be back at the uni in September for my re-sits.'

Nicola looked at him in concern. 'Velsford,' she said reproachfully, 'you didn't tell me you had to re-sit.'

He shrugged and didn't quite meet her eyes. 'It's no big deal. If they throw me out, I'll borrow the money for one of those round the world tickets and just take off.'

'That sounds brilliant,' Teresa said in admiration, her attention diverted for a moment from the ominous sound of his plans for the rest of the summer.

'Doesn't it?' her mother agreed dryly. 'The problem is, what happens when the ticket runs out?'

Velsford laughed, his eyes behind the round gold glasses full of the joke against himself. 'That's like winter,' he said. 'You just don't think about it.'

Helen finished her coke with a definitive slurp, and pushed away the large paper cup. 'Getting back to the hall,' she said, 'do you think we'll have it finished by Mum's birthday?'

Velsford turned to Nicola in surprise. 'You didn't tell me you had a birthday coming up.'

Nicola coloured faintly. 'I didn't think about it. When you're my age —'

'Your age, come on! Velsford said forcefully. 'Don't give me any of that crap! Sorry, I mean —'

'We heard you,' Teresa said, grinning. She knew how her mother felt about swearing.

Nothing could hold Velsford back, however. His face lit up with the familiar enthusiasm. 'We'll have a party.' He nudged Helen, who was sitting nearest. 'Can't we? We'll organise it, you, me and Teresa. We can invite some of my friends that you've met, Chris and Dave and people, and of course all your mum's friends too.'

'Oh no,' Teresa interrupted, shocked. 'Mum never has a

96

party. She just likes to have a quiet time, a meal out or something –'

'I wish you'd all stop talking as if I wasn't here,' Nicola said waspishly. 'I'd love a party, I really would. But I'm not going to have Velsford doing all the hard work for it. It should be our party this time, Velsford,' she said, turning to him with a smile. 'You can't hog all the hospitality, you know. Let it be our party, and you can be top of the guest list.'

Velsford stirred restlessly in his seat. 'Okay,' he said reluctantly. 'But if you need help with anything, just give me a yell, all right? When exactly is your birthday, anyway?'

'August the fifth,' said Nicola. 'I'll be forty-something. Two or three, I have to stop and think which. Two.'

'Forty-two,' said Velsford. Suddenly he reached across the table to clip her cup with his own. He looked at her earnestly. 'I think it's going to be very good year for you. I mean that.'

'Thank you,' said Nicola quietly. She looked at him for rather a long time and Teresa, who was watching jealously, was relieved when Helen broke in with, 'But we still haven't decided anything about the party!'

In spite of what had just been agreed, Velsford immediately launched into a discussion of the best drinks and music, the food and the final touches, that in his opinion made any party worth the name. With every point he made, it was Teresa he appealed to: 'You'll back me up on this one, won't you?'

Confused and uncertain, Teresa kept up an appearance of pleasure, joining in the conversation eagerly. The only sign of her real feelings came in her prompt rejection of any suggestion her mother made, even if at another time she might have agreed with her.

Helen let the talk wash over her. Half-listening,

half-musing on thoughts of her own, she turned to look out across the wall of plants that divided the café from the main part of the store. The place was full of families, struggling to manoeuvre trolleys loaded with lengths of wood, carrying rolls of wallpaper, pausing to interpret figures scrawled on the backs of envelopes. She saw one family where the father was brown, the two small children pale coffee-coloured. She thinks we're just like them, Helen thought, interpreting the white mother's glance in their direction. She thinks we're a family too. Maybe we are, in a way. Maybe we're not so unusual.

She turned back to see Teresa's hand swinging in Velsford's, her mother looking flushed and happy. He's in love with all of us, Helen thought suddenly. All of us, the family. If nothing happens to change that, everything will be all right.

Chapter Nine

'I wish he wasn't coming,' Helen said.

She was lying in bed, watching the sunlight leak into the room round the edges of the curtains. It was about ten o'clock in the morning on the first day of the summer holidays. Even Mum wasn't up yet.

Teresa turned the page of her paperback and glanced across impatiently. 'Well, he is, so you'll just have to put up with it. And remember, we're not telling him anything about your exam results, and we're not saying anything about Velsford.'

'What do you think I am, stupid?' Helen said scornfully. 'I worked that one out for myself ages ago.' She rolled over and reached down for her t-shirt to put on. 'I'm not worried about anything,' she added unconvincingly. 'It'll just be boring, that's all.'

But it took all the pleasure out of seeing Velsford arrive with his borrowed step-ladder and scrapers. Mum and Teresa, still finishing breakfast, greeted him with offers of toast and coffee. He sat down with them for a while, and Helen wandered around the room looking for the scissors to finish off a paper sculpture she had started the evening before.

'They'll be wherever it was you left them,' Nicola said, when appealed to. 'Try and think back, Lennie. You were working on the floor in front of the television, weren't you?'

'She probably took them up to the loo with her,' Teresa

told Velsford. 'We find all sorts of things there. Comics, tea-towels —'

'The tea-towel was only *once*,' Helen said, dangerously close to losing her temper. 'It was in my hand when I went upstairs, that's all.'

'So what stopped you bringing it downstairs again?'

'Teresa, please,' Nicola intervened. 'Helen, if you really can't find the paper scissors, you can use the ones out of my sewing basket just this once.'

'Thanks,' said Helen in an injured voice, throwing a parting glare at Teresa.

But when she had the scissors, she found she didn't really want to use them. She pushed the bits she had cut out, and the bits she had already glued, in a small heap round the back of the sofa, and came back to the table. The others were just getting to their feet.

'Can I have a go at this scraping?' Teresa was saying.

'I want to,' Helen said promptly.

Nicola sighed. 'Well, I'm going to strip the beds,' she said. 'If you two both want to help, you'll have to share a scraper. Velsford, I'll leave it to you to sort out, but if they give you any hassle, I'll send them both out to the supermarket.'

Teresa pulled a face behind her mother's back. 'You Have Been Warned,' she said, in a voice like the narrator of a horror film.

Velsford laughed, which made Helen cross. They were getting on much too well this morning for her liking.

'Okay!'

As soon as Nicola had gone upstairs to start on the bedrooms, Velsford rubbed his hands and grinned round at both of them.

'Who's got a ghetto blaster?' he demanded. 'We can't get started on this job without some music.'

'Me, I'll get it,' said Teresa.

While Teresa was upstairs, Helen looked at Velsford. He was wearing an old t-shirt and baggy blue dungarees, with a tattered baseball cap turned backwards on his head.

'You look funny, dressed like that,' she complained.

'I'll look even funnier when I'm covered in bits of wallpaper,' he said. 'Come on, are you going to have a go? First strike on the wall goes to Helen Flynn!'

Helen picked up the scraper and tried it against the wall. A small shaving of paper curled off and fell onto the old sheets that Velsford had thrown over the carpet.

'You'll have to go at it a lot harder than that, if you want to get it finished this century,' he said with a laugh. His hand clamped over hers and pushed at the scraper. 'See? That's how you do it.'

Helen dodged the long strip of wallpaper that fell towards her toes, and looked back at the wall. There was a long whitish gash in the paper now, looking horrible, like vandalism. The noise of the scraper set her teeth on edge, as Velsford forced her hand into a second stroke.

'That's it,' he said. 'You've got it.'

But some part of Helen protested. What was wrong with the old wallpaper anyway?

'Here we are!' called Teresa from the top of the stairs. Helen was rather annoyed to see that she had changed clothes to look like Velsford, wearing her oldest top, and the dungarees that had lurked at the back of her wardrobe ever since her mother bought them. She brought down the portable stereo and plugged it in.

'It had better be Radio One, since we're workmen,' she said, looking up at Velsford with flirtatious eyes.

She picked up the other scraper and started in the corner by the front door. She went at it energetically, showering the sheet under her feet with red and gold shavings. The wall was beginning to look like something in an

101

abandoned house. Velsford turned to Helen apologetically.

'Oh, you have it,' Helen said, shoving the scraper into his hand. 'I don't really like this part of it, anyway.'

She sat down on the stairs to watch, as Velsford joined Teresa at the bottom of the hall. They stood back to back, scraping and chatting with animation. Whenever a good energetic tune came on the radio, Velsford started to sing in a loud, slightly flat voice, bumping against Teresa to make her laugh. Helen watched their clowning with increasing irritation. She didn't want to join in, yet she couldn't help feeling left out. She was restless and somehow sleepy, with the sort of oppressive feeling she got before an exam. It drove her at last to her feet.

'Tell Mum I've gone out,' she said, as she slid past them to the front door. 'Tell her I've gone to the beach.'

'Will do,' said Teresa, and promptly forgot Helen the moment the door was closed.

While Helen could not shake off the thought of Dad's coming visit, Teresa found it very easy to forget. It took a week to paint the hall, during which time she spent all day and most of her evenings with Velsford. They were rarely on their own; Helen hung round in a maddening fashion, and even in the evenings, when once or twice she managed to shake her off and go round to Velsford's unaccompanied, his university friends were always there, Chris and Dave and others.

She could never be sure of his feelings. He clowned and joked so much that she sometimes thought she was no different from Helen as far as he was concerned. But then sometimes there was a sweetness in the way he looked at her that thrilled her to the centre. She, in return, loved to look at him while he was working beside her, and a casual touch of his hand brought her a shock of delight.

Nicola took little part in the painting, confining herself

102

to providing mugs of tea and plenty of encouragement. When she came to inspect their progress and lingered to chat, Teresa watched her and Velsford with self-conscious misery. Sometimes she felt excluded because they talked as two adults together, from a vantage point she could not yet reach. At other times, what was worse was to see in Velsford an almost boyish admiration for her mother's maturity.

One evening Nicola came round to Velsford's, and it made Teresa rather sick to see the interest the students took in her, particularly the boys. There was no doubt she was attractive, and they seemed to feel the same sort of privilege in hearing her talk about her years of teaching abroad, and her experience of Ireland, as Teresa had felt in listening to their stories and gossip from the Student Union bar.

The hall was finished the day before their father was due to arrive.

'It's a wonderful job,' Nicola said admiringly, as they took up the dust sheets and hoovered the carpet. 'You two should think about going into the profession.'

'What about me?' Helen yelled from the top of the stairs, where she was inspecting her own favourite patch of apricot silk emulsion, a rather tricky bit around the top of the bannister that had taken her ages to get right, resisting all offers of help, even from Velsford.

'Oh, you especially,' Nicola said, grinning at the others. 'As a matter of fact, I've got a proposition to make to the workforce. If everyone's agreeable, I'd like to treat you all to a trip to the cinema.'

'Ace!' Helen exclaimed. But Teresa, turning automatically to Velsford, saw that he was embarrassed.

'I wish you'd told me earlier,' he said. 'I've arranged to go out with some friends. Nothing special, only one of them, Louise, isn't on the phone, so I can't really cancel.'

'Of course you mustn't,' said Nicola. If she was disappointed, she didn't show it, giving him what Teresa interpreted rather resentfully as a sophisticated-woman-amused-by-family-outing look. 'There'll be plenty of other chances to eat ice-cream and throw popcorn, I expect.'

'No, there won't,' Helen said, coming downstairs. 'Dad'll be here tomorrow, and we'll have to spend all our time with him.'

Nicola held out an arm to comfort her. 'Never mind, it's only for a week or ten days. Well, bearing in mind that you can never be a hundred per cent sure of anything with your father.'

Velsford unplugged the hoover, and began to wind up the flex in careful coils. He seemed unsure exactly what to say.

'I can see you're not exactly looking forward to it,' he began eventually, looking round at all of them.

Teresa opened her mouth to deny this, but found she couldn't.

'What's your dad like?' Helen asked, lacing her arm through his. 'You never talk about him, only your mum.'

Velsford smiled at her edgily. 'That's because I haven't seen him since I was about fifteen. When I was thirteen I had to throw him out of the house, and we never really got on after that.'

'Why, what happened?' Teresa asked, adding quickly, as Velsford looked uncomfortable; 'But don't tell us if you don't want to.'

'No, it's okay,' Velsford said. 'He just used to drink too much, that's all, and when he got drunk, he got nasty. He used to take it out on my mum in a big way, like hitting her and shouting and swearing, blaming her for things that weren't her fault. So I stopped him, that's all. I got him on his own when he was almost falling down with the booze,

104

and I threw him out of the house. After that, he came back, but pretty soon my mum got fed up and got a solicitor and stuff, and they separated. My sisters still see him, but I don't. I remember what he was like.'

There was an awkward silence until Teresa said in a flat harsh voice, 'So our dad is just like yours, only without the drink.'

As a celebration of finishing the decorating, the trip to the cinema was not much of a success. Helen was clingy, insisting on sitting with her arm round her mother most of the time, while Teresa quickly decided that the film was rubbish and spent the rest of it sniggering and whispering scornful criticisms.

'That bit when they switched briefcases was pathetic. I saw it coming a mile off, didn't you, Mum?' she demanded as they got into the car afterwards.

'Sorry, dear?' Nicola focused on her daughter with some difficulty. 'Which bit was that, exactly?'

'You can't have been watching at all if you don't remember that bit,' Teresa said in disgust.

'I'm afraid I did have a problem concentrating,' Nicola admitted.

'That man behind us with the giant packet of crisps didn't help,' Helen pointed out. 'And as soon as he'd finished those he went on to those sweets with the rustling wrappers.'

'It's absolutely stupid,' Teresa said. 'They ban people from smoking, yet that doesn't cause nearly as much annoyance as eating sweets does.'

'Huh, you've changed your tune,' Helen said sarcastically. 'I can't imagine what's happened to change your mind — or should I say who?'

Teresa slewed round in her seat. 'God, you think you're so clever,' she said with withering scorn. 'I still disapprove of smoking, of course I do. I just don't think smokers should be persecuted, that's all.'

'One particular smoker, you mean.'

'*Please*,' said their mother. 'Can't we change the subject?'

But nobody seemed really to want to talk. They travelled in silence through the darkening streets until Nicola said, abandoning all pretence that it was a normal evening, 'What time is he arriving tomorrow?'

'The letter only said afternoon,' Teresa replied. 'He said he'd probably take us out to Sandburn.'

Helen groaned. 'That'll be exciting. We've only been there about a million times.'

'I don't think he meant it to be exciting,' Teresa said defensively. 'It's just something to fill up the afternoon. He's got to take us somewhere. Mum's hardly going to let him in the door.'

'Teresa, I never said –' Nicola objected, but Helen was off again before she could finish her sentence.

'Trailing round the Italian Gardens and that stupid nature trail through the woods. And he'll never let us go on the amusements.'

'You never know,' her mother said, trying to keep her tone light. 'Tomorrow might be your lucky day.'

Helen shook her head. 'Fat chance. The most I expect to get out of it is an ice-cream, and I bet I don't even get to choose that myself.'

When they got home, Helen said she couldn't possibly go to sleep without having a drink of hot chocolate, but there wasn't enough milk left. When Nicola pointed out that it was the middle of the summer and a cold drink might be better, Helen burst into tears.

'Teresa always gets everything *she* wants,' she sobbed. 'I bet if it was for her, you'd go to one of those late night shops and get some.'

''Course she wouldn't,' Teresa said impatiently. 'What's the matter with you?'

'We all know what's the matter with her,' Nicola said gently. 'The same thing that's the matter with all three of us. Helen, I'll borrow some milk from the neighbours, and you can change into your pyjamas and drink it down here while Teresa and I clear up and put away the supper things.'

It was rather peaceful, the silence, Teresa thought, as she dried the plates her mother was washing, and put them away in the cupboard. Helen sat at the table, just in view, stirring her hot chocolate and still sniffing occasionally. It was a sort of lull, an easing of the pressure, that made hope plausible.

'Do you remember the time Dad went to teach on that Arvon course, and brought back that giant box of chocolates?' Teresa said. 'I wonder what he'll bring us from Ireland.'

'I remember those chocolates,' Helen said. 'Dad wouldn't give me any pocket money after we got those, because he said there were already enough sweets in the house. And when I complained to Mum, he threw my money box against the wall and broke it.'

Nicola put her hand on the back of Helen's neck and massaged it gently. 'It'll be all right tomorrow,' she said. 'Promise.'

When the doorbell rang next day, just after lunch, the two girls on a shared nervous impulse, rushed straight out the back door into the yard. But when they came back in, giggling sheepishly, their mother was still alone.

'It was only Dorothy from next door wanting her jug back,' she said.

Helen mooched around the room with her hands in her shorts pockets, unable to settle to anything. Teresa picked

107

up a magazine and tried to read. Ten minutes later, the doorbell rang again.

'One of you go,' Nicola said, looking up from her book. 'Teresa?'

It was him this time. She knew it had to be, but it was still a shock to open the door and see him standing there.

'Hello, Dad,' she said.

'Hello, my love.'

Reaching forward, he took her face in both hands and kissed her forehead. His skin was reddish and smooth, and smelt of aftershave. When he stood back she saw he was wearing a tie. For some reason that upset her; suddenly she felt as if she was going to cry. He was smiling nervously. His hands, back in his pockets, fidgeted with his loose change.

'I suppose it's all right to come in?' he said.

'Sorry. Of course it is.' Teresa backed into the hall, making room for him to follow. When she had to turn, she looked back at him over her shoulder.

'Helen's in the living room,' she said. By the time she had decided it was okay to mention her mother, they were already in the room.

'Helen, you're looking very well,' he said warmly, crossing to where she was standing and kissing her on the lips.

'Hello, Dad,' Helen said. As soon as he turned away, she unconsciously wiped her mouth, and moved to stand closer to Teresa. Her father had approached Nicola now, and she was standing up, holding her book in front of her with both hands like a shield. He pushed his head forward, as if he meant to kiss her too, but she moved slightly so that they did not connect.

'Hello, Stephen,' she said quietly. 'Did you have a pleasant journey?'

He gave the familiar stiff nod. His smile had

disappeared; he looked puzzled, disappointed. 'Will you shake hands with me at least?' he said.

'Of course, if you want me to,' said Nicola evenly. She came forward and took his hand in a quick firm grip. 'I hope you'll be comfortable in the old place,' she continued. 'I'm afraid we didn't leave very much in the way of furniture for you.'

'I'll manage,' he said.

There was a short awkward silence. Everyone was still standing up, like they were strangers.

'Some time while you're here, I'd like to talk to you about the money side of things,' Nicola said eventually. 'Unpleasant, I know, but we have to try.' She smiled and made an effort to lighten her tone. 'I won't make things any more difficult for you than I have to, you know.'

'Apart from leaving me in the first place, you mean?'

Teresa couldn't stand this. 'Dad,' she said urgently, 'if we're going to get to Sandburn at all —'

He turned round, and to her relief, relaxed.

'A short spin in the car would do us all some good,' he said with a smile. He glanced back at Nicola. 'I'll take the girls out for a meal tonight as well. I presume you have no objection.'

Teresa could see her mother wanted to refuse and was searching for a reason, but in the end she only said, with tightened lips, 'Make sure you get them back by nine o'clock, then. Helen's rather tired today. She needs an early night.'

'I'll remind Dad,' Teresa said, anxious now only to get him out of the house.

'As she moved towards the door, her father following, she heard Helen starting to say, 'Actually, Mum, I don't feel very well —' but Nicola cut her off, saying in a reassuring but final voice, 'You'll feel better once you're out in the fresh air. And Teresa will be there with you.' So

Helen trailed unwilling down the hall after them.

When they reached the front door, both girls turned to look back at their mother, who had followed them out.

'What are you doing this afternoon, Mum?' Teresa asked, on a sudden needy impulse.

Nicola smiled. 'I'm going to scrub the kitchen to within an inch of its life,' she said.

It was a short walk to where their father had parked. As soon as he unlocked the doors, Helen dived into the back, leaving Teresa to take the front seat where her mother had always sat on their rare family outings. The car had been standing in the sun and the air inside was uncomfortably hot and close, but Teresa's spirits rose now that she had her father on his own. Really, she had him to herself, for Helen had ducked down as far as her seat belt would allow, and the only sound from the back was the occasional squeak of her bare legs against the vinyl.

'So —' Teresa's father lengthened the word into a sigh. He tapped his fingers on the steering wheel. 'Sandburn it is, then?'

'Yes, please,' said Teresa, determined that the afternoon was going to be a success.

He gave a brief nod, started the car and drove to the end of the street where it joined the coast road.

Teresa wound down the window and sat back, letting the breeze play over her face and watching the beach go by. Now and then she glanced at her father. He should have been a handsome man, with his pale faintly freckled skin, dark blue eyes and his black, almost ringleted hair. But his eyes bulged slightly as if from some permanent inner tension, and his forehead was set in a deep puzzled frown.

She felt an impulse to reach up with her fingers and smooth those lines out of his face; but she knew better than even to try and speak to him while he was driving. He peered forward with his hands too tight on the wheel, his shoulders raised, fighting the gears. He was never very good at reading the road ahead, or anticipating what other drivers meant to do. As they jerked to a sudden halt to let a car in ahead of them, he flushed, then, sensing Teresa's attention, launched into an immediate counter-offensive.

'Your new house isn't in a very pleasant part of town, is it? I'm surprised your mother saw fit to move you there.'

Mentally, Teresa jumped back to a safe distance. 'It's all right,' she said carefully. 'It's not as if we've had to change schools or anything. And we've made friends with some of the neighbours.'

'So you're happy there, are you?' His tone was hostile. 'You and your mother, you're perfectly happy there?'

'Well, *happy* —' Teresa looked round, unsuccessfully, for rescue. 'I only meant it's not as bad as it looks.'

'Because of the neighbours.' The glance he gave her was oddly searching.

'Yes, one or two of them.' Teresa just stopped herself mentioning Velsford by name, and plunged on quickly, 'Dad, what are your neighbours like? Your studio flat sounded brilliant in your letters, just the sort of place I'd like to have when I'm older.'

He nodded, his good humour restored for the moment. 'My landlady,' he said, with slight comic emphasis, 'my landlady, Mrs Rafter, is a fine woman, but she believes her cats should have the run of the place, including my landing and the shared bathroom. She's also a little deaf, so I have the benefit of her television all day. Fortunately, she goes to bed early. Other than that, the place is clean and not expensive, and the other tenants come and go quietly, which is as much as I expect from rented accommodation.'

'I see,' Teresa said. 'And are you able to get much work done?' she asked hesitantly. 'I mean, with the landlady's television, and everything —'

'I have my routine, as I think I wrote to you.' He

signalled to overtake, and accelerated so sharply Teresa averted her eyes from the road. 'I have my routine,' he repeated. 'I start the day with mass at St Joseph's round the corner at seven, and work steadily till one or one thirty. After a break to stretch my legs and get something to eat, I'm back at my desk until at least seven. I cook, watch the news, then I have my walk. I'm in bed without fail by eleven, when I might read a bit or listen to the radio.' He smiled briefly. 'It's an efficient regime. I can recommend it to you.'

Teresa was wounded to the quick. She wanted to ask, 'Aren't you unhappy without us? Aren't you unhappy without *me?*' but of course she didn't dare. Besides, they were already on the outskirts of Sandburn, and Helen was sitting up and looking out of the window.

Sandburn had been a fashionable resort in Victorian times, and the old part of the town, which they were now passing through, had a seedy sort of elegance. Beyond the imposing but slightly shabby fronts of the private hotels, the road zigzagged down the cliffs in a series of hairpin bends to the sandy beach below. To Helen's disappointment and Teresa's relief, their father stopped the car at the top.

'We'll park here and walk down,' he announced, undoing his seat belt.

Helen leaned forward and said to Teresa in an undertone, 'Ask him if we can go down in the cable car.'

Teresa shook her head impatiently, and their father glanced back as he opened the car door.

'Sorry, what was that?'

'Helen needs to go to the loo,' Teresa said.

'No, I don't,' Helen retorted irately.

Their father eyed her with disfavour, but got out of the car without saying more. Helen, feeling sore, cheered up a little once she was out in the warm breezy air. Sandburn was never very crowded, even on a Saturday afternoon, and there were few people on the road in front of them as they walked down.

'Shall we spend a little while on the beach?' her father suggested. Helen, her eyes on the small amusement arcade, suppressed a sigh.

They walked down onto the sand. As soon as she could, Helen went off by herself to clamber around the rocks and stir up the pools between them with a stick of driftwood. The others moved down to the water's edge, from where she could hear her father's voice, lecturing Teresa about shells. When he grew silent, she guessed they were looking for flat stones to skim with. That was all her father ever wanted to do at the beach, skim stones like he used to as a boy in Ireland. Helen let go of her stick and stood up to watch him as he bent with a stone in his hand then, with a sudden flick, tossed it out across the sparkling sea to skip four or five times before it sank. Teresa tried next, but she had never learnt the knack; the stone slipped out of her hand and fell with a splash.

'I can do that!' Helen called across to them. She started walking quickly across the wet sand. 'I can do it,' she repeated as they stood and watched her. She stooped and found a good stone, one of the flat, smooth, slate-coloured ones, and stood for a moment, weighing it in her hand and looking out across the water. When it felt ready, she let it go. It hopped once, twice, three times before disappearing into a wave.

'Very good,' said Teresa, genuinely impressed. 'I didn't know you could do that.'

Helen shrugged modestly. She glanced towards her father, but he was already bending down to look for more stones.

'I'll show you how it's done, Teresa,' he said when he straightened up. 'You're not holding your wrist the right way, that's all.'

He took hold of her hand to show her. Helen prodded the ground with her toe for a minute, then wandered away. She was more interested in the rocks, she told herself. There might be a starfish in one of those pools, and if there was, she wasn't going to tell *anybody*.

Eventually, they left the beach and walked inland towards the woods and the Italian Gardens. Helen ran ahead of them a little way, trying to jump from the shadow of one tree to another without stepping in the hot sunshine. On the grass near the little stream, families were picnicking and young children scooped at the water with nets on poles, hoping to catch a fish.

Teresa and her father walked slowly, talking about school and Teresa's GCSE options. Helen was busy pretending she was on her own. She began a story in her head about being the leader of a gang of human survivors in a world run by robots. Teresa and Dad were both robots, that was it, and they thought she was one of them, but she wasn't. She was gathering information for the resistance, only she had to be careful what she said or they would realise she wasn't on their side.

'Look at those humans putting food into their mouths, isn't it revolting?' she said as Teresa caught her up. 'Aren't you glad we don't need such messy and disgusting ways of getting energy?'

'What are you on about?' Teresa said good-humouredly. She was feeling much better after hearing Dad praise her exam results. He came up on the other side of Helen and dropped a heavy hand on her shoulder.

'And how are you getting on at school? You never write to me, so I never know what's happening at all.'

'It's going all right,' Helen said, looking away from him and feeling as if she couldn't breathe.

'You got your hundred metres swimming certificate this

114

term, didn't you, Lennie?' Teresa said, trying to help.

'Oh, that's grand,' said their father heartily.

'Bags I'm first in the Gardens,' Helen shouted, breaking away from them again.

Their father liked the Italian Gardens, where the flowers were all marshalled into formal designs, disciplined by box hedges. At one end was the Floral Clock, laid out in memory of an alderman, and at the other a topiary walk. This contained trees trained and clipped into all kinds of shapes of solid geometry, and one was rumoured to resemble a teddy bear, though the girls had never agreed on which. Their father walked round slowly, inspecting the trees from every angle.

'Sure, it's very fine,' he said with a fantastic laugh. 'An improvement on nature, wouldn't you say?'

Teresa wasn't sure if he was being serious or funny, and since she hated to misunderstand a joke, responded with a smile so subdued he could interpret it any way he wished. Her eye was caught by a tree right in the corner, half-hidden behind the rest. From the front it had the same disciplined appearance as them, but at the back it was growing unchecked, little green branches shooting out in a way that was somehow more shocking than in a natural tree. She did not draw her father's attention to it, but was filled with a sudden longing for her mother to have been there to show it to.

Helen sidled up to her. 'I'm thirsty,' she hissed.

Teresa looked across at her father, who frowned at the distraction and then said with a visible effort, 'Why not, let's have a soft drink or an ice cream. I suppose there's a kiosk nearby.'

There was in fact a tea hut just at the end of the path, with wooden picnic tables and benches, and a lively contingent of wasps. Helen sat down at an empty table while Teresa and her father queued. They brought back lemonade cans with straws and biscuits wrapped in plastic. Helen and her father slurped noisily, while Teresa tore open the biscuit packets with her teeth. They ate and drank without talking, shading their eyes from the sun and looking at the people sitting at the other tables. Eventually Teresa and her father spoke at once.

'How's the book —'

'Are you still —'

'I'm sorry,' Teresa said with a little laugh. 'You first.'

'Are you still going to your ballet classes?' he asked. 'That's all.'

'Yes, I've gone up a grade.' She struggled to think of something more to say about it.

'And what was your question?' he smiled.

'Just about the book.' She felt embarrassed now. She had always despised her mother for asking.

'Oh, it's progressing.' He didn't seem to mind being asked. 'Some small technical difficulties over poisons means I've been spending a lot of time in libraries lately.'

'I suppose it gets you away from the landlady's television,' Teresa ventured.

'I suppose it does.'

Neither of them seemed able to think of any other topic to prolong the conversation. Helen was picking the varnish off the table and swatting at the wasps. After a few minutes' silence, their father sighed and looked at his watch.

'Well, it's after five,' he said. 'I suppose we'd better be heading back.'

On the journey home Teresa sat in the back with Helen. She felt too tired to strain herself to talk, and if her father noticed, he didn't comment. Twenty mintues later they pulled up outside the house.

'Oh, are we going home?' Helen said hopefully.

'It's just somewhere to park,' Teresa muttered.

Their father turned round. 'It's not too early to go and eat, is it? By the time we've walked into the town centre and found a place –'

''Course not,' said Teresa loyally. 'I'm hungry now. Come on, Lennie, undo your seatbelt.'

They scrambled out and waited on the pavement while their father checked the car was locked and then got out his wallet and checked the money it it. Helen looked longingly towards her own front door. She whispered to Teresa, 'Can't I just go and say hello to Mum? I won't be two ticks.'

'No, he's ready,' Teresa said in a louder voice, as their father turned towards them.

'Shall we go?' His smile was more dutiful than enthusiastic. He walked towards them with his arms held out, as if expecting to take a daughter on either side, but Helen executed a neat sidestep so that Teresa was the one caught in the middle. They walked as far as the High Street before anyone spoke.

'Where are we going to eat?' Helen demanded.

'Well, not here, for a start,' Teresa said, coming to a stop outside the Red Lion Hotel and looking at their menu scornfully. 'Florida cocktail, steak and salad for £6.99! Why don't they just say grapefruit? Everybody knows that's what it means.'

'Does it?' Helen asked. 'How do you know? Maybe it means strawberries and passion fruit. Maybe it's a drink. How do you know it isn't a drink?'

'Because it isn't,' Teresa said impatiently. 'Everyone knows they mean grapefruit. Oh, sorry, Dad, we're coming,' she added in alarm, as their father turned and walked on. As they caught up, she hissed at Helen, quite unfairly, 'Why do you always have to do that?'

But Helen didn't care. She had seen a restaurant coming

up ahead of them, and said excitedly, 'Look, it's Dear Friends. We went there for Catriona's birthday, and it was really brilliant. Ask Dad if we can go there, Teresa.'

'You ask him,' Teresa retorted. But he was slowing up in any case.

'Dear Friends Chinese Restaurant,' he read out. 'That sounds like a good omen, ha-ha.'

'Oh, yes please,' Helen said eagerly. 'It's a brilliant place, Dad, honestly.'

Teresa inspected the menu. 'It looks all right,' she said cautiously. 'Not too expensive.'

Her father pressed her shoulder lightly. 'I'm really not so broke you need worry,' he said. 'If you like it, we'll go in.'

'Let's,' Teresa said with pleasure. She felt proud as she followed him up the stairs. With his longish curly hair and his crumpled linen jacket he looked like a poet or an adventurer; at that moment she wouldn't have swapped him for anyone else in the world.

The good mood continued while they were sitting down waiting to order. Their father started to laugh as he opened his menu, pages and pages of it.

'They have the same little drawings on every Chinese menu I've ever seen,' he said. 'I suppose there must be a factory in Peking, printing all the Chinese menus for all the Chinese restaurants in the world.'

'But there's only one tape,' Helen said. 'You just listen. The same songs go round and round.'

'Well, that's the trouble with Chinese music,' Teresa said. 'You listen to a song and two hours later you want to listen to it again.'

Helen looked at her blankly. 'I don't get it.'

'Never mind,' said Teresa. 'Let's decide what we're going to have.'

Helen scanned the menu, and giggled. 'Look, Tess, number fifty-five. Braised groper!'

Her father looked up, frowning. 'Is that what you'd like?' he asked abruptly.

Helen looked at him, rapidly losing confidence in her joke. 'No, it's funny, that's all. Well, I thought it was funny.' She buried herself in the menu again, not speaking until the waiter came for their order.

Their father had ordered a bottle of white wine to go with the food, and when it arrived, he seemed to relax again.

'Now tomorrow,' he said, taking a short deep swallow and putting down his glass again, 'we have mass in the morning, of course, but in the afternoon I was hoping you'd give me a hand with some clearing up at the old place. I still have a few things that need sorting and packing, and it might be a good idea to hack down the grass in the garden.' He looked at them humorously. 'It's a terrible time to be selling a house, so the estate agent tells me, but we needn't make it more difficult than we have to.'

'Sure, Dad,' Teresa said with a glance at Helen. 'We'd love to help. And how long are you staying, by the way?'

'Ten days or so,' he replied with a nod.

'So you'll be here for Mum's birthday, then?'

Teresa glared at Helen. She needn't have sounded quite so disappointed.

'That's the idea,' he said with a slightly nervous smile. 'I thought we might make a little occasion of it. You two girls could help me in the planning of it, if you like.'

Teresa kicked Helen hard under the table as she opened her mouth to object. 'Let's talk about it after the weekend,' she suggested. 'We've got a bit of time, after all. So you're really going ahead with selling the house?'

'I am.' His smile broadened. 'I think that's best. I'm still in hopes of us all being settled in Dublin together by next Christmas.'

Helen got to her feet. 'I have to go to the loo,' sh announced unsteadily. 'Don't worry, I know where it is She made her way across the room, disappearing behind carved screen.

When she had gone, Stephen Flynn leaned across t Teresa confidentially. 'I've written to Father McShane, an I'm going to see him after mass tomorrow. I've asked hir to act as intermediary between your mother and myself. I she can be brought to reconsider the harm she's done i breaking up the family, and get some counselling about it I'm sure we shall all be together again soon.'

Teresa felt a kind of dread spreading through her body, sickness in the pit of her stomach and a shivery weakness i her arms and legs. She didn't understand, she didn understand; once, she had hoped for this, dreamed of it but now she knew it was all wrong, it was terrible.

'I'm not sure what Mum thinks,' she began in a lov uncertain voice. 'I mean, she does have a choice – and yo sounded quite happy, earlier on, when you were talkin about Dublin.' She swallowed, and came out with it. 'Ar you sure you aren't happier on your own?'

As she spoke, his eyes seemed to bulge even mor prominently in his head, and for one dreadful moment Teresa thought he was going to hit her. Then his han unclenched and returned to his lap.

'It's not a question of happiness,' he said with freezin calm. 'It's a question of what's right.'

Helen came back then, followed immediately by th waiter with the food. Teresa spooned rice onto her plate and passed the dishes round, her face set against tears Helen, for some reason, seemed to have cheered u considerably.

'Wow, this is excellent,' she said chattily. 'There's onl one sort of cooking that's better, and that's Indian, isn't it Teresa?'

Her father smiled edgily. 'We could have gone to an Indian restaurant if you'd wanted,' he said. 'I thought you were keen to come here.'

'Oh no, I mean Indian food cooked at home,' Helen said. 'I've learnt how to cook it, haven't I, Teresa?'

'One dish,' Teresa said grudgingly, wondering where this was leading.

'You learnt that at school, I suppose,' their father said.

'No, at home,' Helen said casually. 'It's just something I do for fun with Velsford.'

Teresa glared at her but it was too late. Her father contracted his brow.

'Velsford? I don't think I've heard that name.'

'He's a friend of Mum's and ours,' Helen said. 'He's giving Mum a party for her birthday.'

Teresa saw her father becoming very still.

'And does he live with you?'

'Of course not,' Teresa said loudly, before Helen could continue. 'He's only a young student, he lives round the corner from us, and Mum paid him to do some decorating, so we all got friendly. He's really more our friend than Mum's, isn't he, Helen?' But for all her glaring, Helen wouldn't fall in line.

'I don't know,' she said in a thoughtful voice. 'Mum really likes him. And I know Velsford really likes her.'

Their father said nothing more, but began to eat rapidly. Teresa pushed her plate away, having lost all appetite. She looked at Helen in cold fury, and wondered what game she was playing. But Helen only hitched up her chin and went on eating her dinner with visible enjoyment.

It was a relief all round, so it seemed, when they parted company outside the house an hour later.

'I'll come tomorrow to go with you to eleven o'clock mass,' their father said. 'Your mother will, I trust, come with us.'

'I expect so,' Teresa said tiredly.

'Good.' He gave an earnest nod. 'I'll see you all tomorrow, then. Goodnight!' He went off without trying to kiss either of them, striding away down the road as if he wanted to be somewhere else.

Their mother, who had been watching television, got up and turned it off as they came in.

'So how did it go,' she asked, turning to face them. 'Was it nice food, Helen? Where did you eat in the end?'

'The Chinese place on the High Street, but Mum,' Helen rushed up to her, hot-faced, 'he says he's going to take us back to Ireland!'

Nicola gathered her into a hug. 'Of course he isn't,' she said strongly. 'Of course he isn't.'

She looked across at Teresa. 'Did he really say that?'

Reluctantly, Teresa nodded. 'He's going to see Father McShane. He wants him to try to bring you both back together.'

To her surprise, Nicola started to laugh. 'Poor Father McShane. I'd better let him know I'm not expecting him to do any such thing.'

'Helen didn't help,' Teresa said, growing rather resentful of the cuddling that was going on. 'She kept going on and on about Velsford, giving Dad absolutely the wrong idea, when I told her not to even mention him.'

'Why ever shouldn't she?' Nicola demanded. 'Oh, I see. Well, if he got hold of the wrong end of the stick, that's his problem.'

'I wanted him to,' Helen said with satisfaction. 'I wanted him to know he's not needed.'

As Nicola started to laugh, it was all suddenly too much for Teresa. The disappointments and confusion of the day were brought to a head, seeing Helen and her mother giggling together.

'Well, why did you marry him in the first place, if you hate him so much?' she shouted, and ran out of the room, banging the door.

Chapter Ten

She lay under the duvet, waiting for Helen to come up so she could pretend to be asleep. She knew they were talking about her downstairs, but she didn't care. They were probably talking about Dad too, laughing at what a joke it was that he still wanted them back. Nobody cared about him, Teresa thought fiercely. Nobody thought about what he might be feeling.

She stiffened as she heard footsteps come upstairs to the door, Helen coming to bed at last. But when the door opened she saw in the half-light that it wasn't Helen after all, it was her mother.

'I've put Helen to bed on the sofa downstairs,' she said, coming in. 'It's been a difficult day for her.'

Always Helen, Teresa thought bitterly. She continued to lie hunched under the bedclothes as her mother approached.

'I think we need to talk,' Nicola said. She sat down on the edge of the bed, trapping the duvet near Teresa's feet. Feeling her there was obscurely comforting. Teresa remembered how she used to come and sit for a few minutes after bedtime, especially if there had been any trouble during the day. Not much was ever said; not much could safely be said in those days with Dad at home.

'Mum,' she said hesitantly.

'Yes, love.'

'Why did you marry him?'

She felt, more than heard, her mother sigh. 'He was different when I first met him. Well, you know that.

You've asked me before how we met.'

'Tell me again,' Teresa said. 'Tell me what happened.'

'Well, we met in Italy, in a small town near Genoa, where we were both teaching in a language school. I'd gone out there to get away from home, after a nasty break-up with a boyfriend. Your father was trying to earn some money and write up his PhD at the same time. He never did finish it.'

Teresa moved so she could see the outline of her mother's head. It was too dark to see her expression. 'Did you like him straight away?'

'Yes, sort of. He seemed rather silly and sweet. He didn't take the teaching at all seriously and he hardly looked at his thesis. It was as though the whole thing, Italy, the school, even me, was a holiday from reality for him. I didn't think that at the time, of course; I suppose I was happy to join him. I knew he wanted to be a writer and that impressed me very much. Neither of us was earning much and we would spend hours over a cup of coffee in the café near the school, studying the locals and talking about the future and what we wanted out of life. I seem to remember the other teachers at the school were older, already settled with families or whatever, so we were thrown together a lot. We certainly didn't learn much Italian, which seems a pity.'

'And he asked you to marry him?'

'Yes, we got engaged after six months. I was surprised, because I hadn't even been sure we were going out together, not properly; I mean, we hardly even kissed. Anyway, I felt — I don't know, of course it was wrong, quite wrong, but I felt I would be going back to England with my head held high. I could show my family and friends, and most of all my mother, that I'd been able to get somebody else. It was all for the wrong reasons. I don't know what was going through your father's head. Maybe

125

he was trying to hold on to Italy.'

'Maybe he loved you,' Teresa said.

'Maybe,' her mother agreed. 'I'm sure he thought he did. And I was in love with him. I wanted to love him. I wanted everything to be wonderful, the wedding, the house, the babies. The plan originally was that we were going to settle in Dublin. I went over to meet his family, and that's when I started to get uneasy. Stephen was different on his home ground. He was distant, closed in on himself, and when I saw him with his parents I was almost frightened. There was such a terrible atmosphere in their house, a sort of suppressed rage between them all. And Stephen wouldn't talk to me any more, or tell me what he was thinking. I asked him if he was having second thoughts and he said of course not, was I?'

'And were you?' Teresa asked.

Her mother was silent. 'I think, if I'd been less unsure of myself, I'd have postponed the wedding,' she said at last. 'But when I tried to talk to my mother about it, she went bananas. What, cancel all the arrangements? Write to all our friends and relatives and return the presents? The humiliation would have killed her. She told me your father was just suffering from pre-marriage nerves, and so was I. So I went ahead with it.' She squeezed Teresa's knee. 'And you've been around for most of the rest of it.'

'But wasn't it all right for even some of the time?' Teresa asked hopefully. 'I mean, before Helen came along and he started hitting you?' It shocked her to say it so directly.

Her mother leant back. She shook her head. 'No, it was never very good. It was as if −' she paused. 'It was as if nothing touched him except his work. He never felt he had to explain anything to me. If his writing was going badly, if he was worried about money, I just had to guess. It worked the other way too. When I was pregnant with you I became unbearable to live with, absolute hell for anybody,

126

I was so irritable and moody. Something to do with hormones, I suppose, though it didn't happen with Helen. But your father sailed through all of that. He never took offence, it didn't trouble him, and the only reason I can think of is that it didn't touch him. His work was going well and he was happy.

'When Helen was born and had colic so badly she was screaming half the night, what got to your father was the effect it had on his work. And of course, he no longer had much support from me. You were one of those restless active toddlers, yelling blue murder the instant you got bored. I was half dead between the two of you and I simply didn't have the energy left to give to your father too. That's when it started.'

'You should have left him,' Teresa said harshly.

'I did try, once, when you were both small,' her mother said. 'I took the boat to England and went home to my mother, but she wouldn't let me stay. She was afraid of what the priest and her Catholic neighbours would think. In 1982, can you believe it? That's what she said, but looking back, I think she blamed me for not trying hard enough. Her own marriage wasn't particularly happy, but she'd put up with my father for more than thirty years, so why should I escape? Anyway, I got no help from her. I'd lived in Ireland for five years, I had no friends I'd kept in touch with, I wasn't on any council list. So I went back to your father. I couldn't think of anywhere else to go.'

Teresa reached out and touched her hand in the dark.

'I loved him, you see, and I went on hoping —' her mother's voice wavered and cracked. 'I wanted to help him fight it, but he wouldn't even admit there was a problem. And all the time I kept thinking, if only I could do things better, arrange our lives better, he wouldn't get so angry. When we came over to England and I went back to work, things were better for a while. He had more time for his writing and he was getting more successful. But even that didn't help him. And then this year, when he said we should go back to Ireland, something inside me just –'

Nicola broke off in tears. Teresa felt the incurable hurt of it, and tears welled in her own eyes.

'You were right to say no,' she said. 'We couldn't have gone with him.' But it weighed on her to know that, to think of facing her father tomorrow with that knowledge inside her of her mother's hurt.

'But in Italy it was good,' she protested suddenly. 'You said it was good then.'

'It was.' Her mother wiped her eyes with the back of her hand. 'That's what I hung on to, through all the rest of it. That's what I hoped one day we'd get back to. But I waited too long, Tess. I couldn't wait any more.' She moved off the bed, and stood up.

'I'm sorry, Tess. I should be letting you get to sleep instead of burdening you with all of this.'

'That's all right,' Teresa said quietly.

'Oh, one nice thing happened today,' her mother continued, struggling back into her normal voice. 'Velsford called round to see how we were getting on. He had a girl with him.'

'A girl?'

'Someone from the university. Louise, I think her name was. She seemed very nice.'

'Great,' Teresa said tonelessly. She lay back in bed. It was anything but good news, but she couldn't worry about it now.

'Goodnight, then, love,' said her mother. 'See you in the morning.'

Teresa waited until the door was shut before allowing herself to cry.

Walking into church with her father and mother the

following morning, Teresa felt hollow, emptied. On the short walk to church, her parents had scarcely spoken. Her mother, white-faced and determined, kept hold of Helen's hand all the way, and whenever Helen made a remark, bent protectively to listen. Their father wore a faint impermeable smile, as if appearing in public with the family was in itself a victory. He led the way to the front of the church, to one of the pews left empty by those arriving earlier. Teresa could see some of the adults in the congregation taking note as they all filed down to the front. Once in the pew, she knelt down beside her father for a minute, but she could not pray. She did not know what to pray for.

When the priest and the altar boys came out, she stood and mechanically joined in the opening hymn. She sat for the readings, stood for the Gospel, sat again for the sermon, stood once more for the creed; none of it touched her. Her mother's quiet voice and her father's louder one both reached her as if slightly out of step with the congregation. At the offertory her father, singing the hymn in his pleasant baritone, put a twenty-pound note in the collection.

Teresa bent her head, summoning what quietness she could during the consecration. Then it was time to go up to the altar. After communion, the final blessing, the final hymn; Father McShane and the altar boys genuflected and left by the door to the sacristy. The congregation sat or knelt forward for a moment, then began to straggle out of church. Stephen Flynn knelt in the pew, his face hidden by his clasped hands.

'Are we going now?' Helen demanded in a low voice.

'Not yet, darling,' said her mother. 'Remember, we have to see Father McShane.'

'What, all of us?'

'Just Mum and Dad, stupid,' said Teresa.

The church was almost empty when their father rose to his feet. He glanced along the pew.

'Shall we go?'

'Stephen,' Nicola said firmly, 'I phoned Father McShane this morning and asked if he would see us after mass. I believe he's waiting for us in the sacristy.'

Their father frowned. 'I wanted to see him,' he began, 'but I don't see the need for any immediate consultation –'

'You will,' said Nicola a little grimly. 'Come on, Stephen. Let's not keep the poor man waiting.'

Helen and Teresa slid together along the varnished wooden pew and watched their parents cross to the vestry door. The altar boys were just coming out; they halted in surprise to see people still in the church so long after the service, then hurried on out into the sunshine. The noise of the door closing behind them echoed in the cold polish-scented air. After that, there was silence. Teresa studied the flowers on the altar and the stations of the cross. Helen began to read a hymn book. Then suddenly the shouting started. Teresa looked at Helen and looked away. Neither of them spoke.

It was their mother who was shouting. Behind hers, Father McShane's voice started to rise, and then their father's flat and persistent. It went on and on. Teresa wanted to rush outside, to get away; she couldn't stand the sick feeling it gave her. Abruptly it stopped. Teresa waited, her stomach knotted flat, then it began again, their mother speaking in that angry raw voice it hurt to hear.

Suddenly the door opened and their father walked out, looking straight ahead of him, and went quickly down the side aisle to the exit. Teresa stood up, but he did not even look towards her. As the far door banged shut, making an echo round the church, the others came out of the sacristy. Father McShane had an arm round their mother, who was crying, distraught.

'I'm sorry to have to do it to you, Father,' she was saying, 'but I needed a witness. Nobody ever believes the things he says once he gets going, the accusations. And I had to have you to back me up in what I was telling him. He'll take it from a priest, when he won't take my word for anything, ever —'

Helen was running round the church towards her. 'Mum!' She buried her face in her mother's side. 'Mum, he didn't —'

'Of course not,' her mother said. 'Of course not. He wouldn't, not in a church.'

She turned and looked across at Teresa, still standing in the pew. Her red tear-stained eyes were full of apology and concern. Teresa felt a sudden aggressive reaction; she didn't *want* to give the comfort appealed for. For a moment she did nothing. Then, ashamed of her reluctance, she went across the church to put her arm around her mother.

'I said I'd go, so I'm going,' Teresa insisted.

Two hours later, they had finished lunch — salad and cold meat out in the back yard because the day was so hot. The table, graced with a tablecloth, had a festive air.

'But Teresa,' their mother looked at her earnestly, shading her eyes with her hand. 'He'll be feeling very sore after what happened this morning. Don't you think it might be better to leave him to himself?'

'We agreed,' Teresa said. 'I promised I'd go and give him a hand. Helen doesn't have to come if she doesn't want to.'

Helen looked up briefly from the Sunday magazine. 'I don't, actually.'

Nicola sighed. 'All right,' she said. She pulled down the shoulders of her top to catch the sun and settled back in her chair. 'Do what you think's best, Teresa. But come back here at once if there's any hint of trouble, hear me?'

'There won't be,' Teresa said flatly.

'Well, be careful.' Nicola went on looking at her as if she wanted to say more, but when Teresa sighed impatiently, she smiled and picked up the newspaper.

'See you later,' Teresa said, and got up to go.

She did not know why she was going, except that a promise was a promise, and somebody had to care about how Dad felt. At first it was pleasant to be out in the Sunday streets, so hot and silent. Nobody was about. They must all be away or indoors, she thought. The alleys were too hot to play in, and even the cats had stopped basking on the bonnets of parked cars and lurked instead, yellow-eyed, in the darkness beneath them.

In a while Teresa too got tired of the glare. She rested a minute in the shade of the big bushes that ran along the side of the railway bridge, and then she was on the main road, breathing the petrol fumes that seemed not to rise in the hot, still, air, but linger at car level. It was a long way past the closed shops and the big white house to her turning. The pavement struck up through the thin soles of her sandals, and the flints in the pavement sparked in the sun so that when she blinked there were hot coloured points behind her eyes. When she reached the house at last, she was thirsty and tired and out of temper with herself, almost forgetful of the impulse that had sent her out there.

She opened the gate and walked up to the front door. She rang the bell and, while waiting for her father to let her in, she turned and looked back along the path to the gate. The garden was parched looking, with brown patches on the lawn. Some of the lilies, top-heavy, had flopped forward, and weeds were beginning to show. Then the door behind her opened, and she spun round to see her father. He had changed into old clothes, a faded blue shirt and canvas jeans. His face looked strained and suspicious.

'I didn't know if you'd come,' he said.

'Oh, I always meant to come,' Teresa said, trying to smile. She followed him into the cool dark hall, smelling of dust and cardboard. Empty boxes were piled precariously next to the bookcase and on top of the telephone table.

'Would you like a drink of some kind?' he said. 'I can offer you fizzy water, or tea. Or milk, I suppose.'

'Fizzy water would be great,' Teresa said gratefully.

While he was fetching it from the kitchen she took a look in at the open doorway of the living room. He had pinned up a bedspread at the window instead of a curtain, and had plugged his clock radio next to the air bed. Against the far wall was his suitcase, the lid flung back to reveal the rummaged contents. It was strange to think of him living like a squatter in the house with the shapes of the missing furniture outlined on the walls like ghosts.

'Here you are.' He was holding a big glass of water. Teresa took it and drank thirstily.

'Wow, that's better!' She smiled at him.

He returned the smile vaguely. 'I was in here,' he said, going ahead of her into the front room. 'I've brought everything together. It's just a matter of sorting it.'

The floor of the front room was covered in books, in piles and lying singly, magazines, folded clothes and oddments. Stephen Flynn looked at it all in silence.

'Is there a lot to do?' Teresa asked

'Well, I've made up my mind about most of it,' he said doubtfully. 'What you could do is go through the magazines and papers. I've marked the articles I want to keep, mostly things I might use for our man Septimus. If you could tear them out, we can throw the rest away.'

'Well, we should take the papers to the recycling point,' Teresa suggested.

133

'Whatever.'

He stooped, picking up a book and weighing it against another as if that would somehow tell him which to save, which to abandon. Teresa went over to the piles of magazines and began to check through them. Most of the articles had some connection with Ireland or medicine or the Church, but there were one or two which surprised her, about the fauna of the Antarctic, or drug smuggling in South America.

They worked in silence, her father slowly filling a box, with long pauses for thought about each book. Suddenly he said, 'I can't understand what your mother said to me in front of the priest today. Can you understand it?'

'I didn't hear it,' Teresa said, feeling like a coward.

He bent over his box of books. 'She said,' he stopped. 'She said I had rights of access to you, not to her. She said I was to observe the limits of the separation agreement, and not imagine the situation was ever going to change in any way. When I turned to the priest and told him what I thought her reasons were for wanting a separation, she seemed to lose control.' He looked at Teresa uneasily. 'Teresa, I don't like to say this to you about your own mother, but I'm beginning to think she's a little round the bend.'

This was so unexpected that Teresa wanted to laugh. 'Dad,' she began. 'How can you say that, when you're the one who —'

But he went on looking at her in that same strange puzzled way, and the words died on her lips. He really meant it. He really didn't understand.

When she said nothing more, her father went back to his sorting and so, eventually, did Teresa. Once or twice she had to fight to stop the tears from welling over onto her cheeks. What had she come for? What had she hoped to achieve? He had no sense of his own failure, no idea that he

134

might be to blame. He would never understand, and that was why Mum had stopped trying. Mixed in with Teresa's grief and disappointment was a bitter little recognition of the fact her mother had been right. She shouldn't have come. She hadn't changed anything.

He was saying something; she hadn't caught the first part of it.

'Sorry, what?' she said, wiping her eyes on the back of her hand.

'The photograph I found this afternoon,' he repeated a little impatiently. 'It fell out of a volume of that old red encyclopaedia. I'll show it to you if you feel like having a good laugh at us both.'

'A picture of you and Mum?' Teresa asked in surprise.

'An old one,' he said. 'Before we were married.'

'Please can I see it?' Teresa said eagerly, getting to her feet and wiping her hands on her shorts.

He smiled, pleased to have her interest again. 'Your mother looks lovely, of course,' he said, pulling it out of the box and bringing it for her to see. 'But I look rather quaint. I hadn't realised how much shirt collars have altered.'

The cardboard frame was battered and dog-eared, but the photograph inside was fresh enough. They were standing against a low wall, under a dark blue sky. Teresa was shocked by how young they looked, and how happy. Her mother's hair was straight and long, and she was wearing a sleeveless dress. Her father, deeply tanned, grinned boyishly into the camera.

'That was in Italy, wasn't it?' Teresa said.

He nodded. 'Your mother and me.' He touched the faces in the photograph with surprising gentleness. Then he said, 'She isn't coming back to me, is she, Tess?'

'No, Dad,' she whispered.

He took the photograph from her, and put it back in the box.

Chapter Eleven

Helen came running into the hall as Teresa came back.

'Mum says we can have a takeaway for supper. I want pizza, so that'd better be what you want!'

Teresa pushed past her without saying anything. Helen danced in her wake chanting, 'Mushrooms and sweetcorn and ham and spicy beef and olives and —'

'Shut up, will you?' Teresa snarled over her shoulder. She went into the kitchen and waited impatiently for her mother to turn round from her coffee-making.

'You're back early,' Nicola said in surprise. 'Was everything okay?'

Teresa shrugged. She didn't trust herself to speak. Her mother looked at her more closely.

'Something's upset you, hasn't it?' She yelled into the living room. 'Helen, turn that wretched thing down, will you? I can hardly hear myself think in here!'

The noise of the television muted, and Nicola said quietly, 'What did he say?'

Teresa leant back against the wall. 'Nothing much,' she said. 'It's just, I don't know — why does everything have to be so awful all the time? Why can't things ever work out?' She turned her head away so that her mother wouldn't see her crying, and felt her mother's arms come round her to comfort her.

'I wish I knew,' Nicola said sadly. 'I really wish I knew.'

A little later, Teresa broke away from the comfort. 'I want to go and see Velsford,' she said, blinking hard, her voice back to normal. 'Is that all right?'

'Of course it is,' Nicola said in surprise. Then, following Teresa's gaze, she added, 'I'm sure I can keep Helen occupied, if that's what you mean. There's a film on later that she's keen to watch.'

Teresa managed a smile. 'Thanks, Mum.'

'But be sensible about it, won't you?' Nicola added, and gently squeezed her arm. 'I mean, if he's studying or he's got company. I worry we take up too much of his time already.'

'Okay,' Teresa said. 'I'll try and be back by ten.'

'But it's only six now,' her mother protested. 'What are you going to do about eating?'

It was no good asking Teresa; she was already halfway out of the house.

She stood, a few minutes later, outside Velsford's door. He was slow answering the bell and she began to wonder if he was at home. The door was closed and she could see nothing through the glass panel but the coat rail and the empty stairs, which rippled as she tilted her head this way and that. Then she caught movement at the upstairs window.

'Velsford?' she called up. 'Is that you?'

She stepped back onto the pavement, trying to see, and in a minute the door was opened. Velsford, looking slightly rumpled in a blue striped t-shirt and jeans, his feet bare, stood looking out at her. Something in his face made her say, 'Oh, sorry, have you been asleep?'

'No.' He was smiling, but still she got the impression he was not quite glad to see her. Perhaps it was only his silence that made her uneasy.

'Can I come in?' she asked.

'Of course,' he said, but he didn't immediately move. 'I didn't expect to see you today,' he continued. 'I thought you'd be out and about with your dad.'

'Not today,' Teresa said. Suddenly she thought, perhaps he's got someone up in his room, and that's why he doesn't want me to come in. Perhaps it's that girl Mum saw him with yesterday.

'Look, if you're busy —' she began in a hurry, but he waved that away.

'Don't be silly. I'm sorry it took me so long to come down, but I though you'd just come straight in. The door's never locked, look.' He showed her the side of the door, where the catch was up. 'Come on in. I've been working, but I could do with a break. And it's always nice to have company on Sunday evenings. God knows they're hard enough, with only Harry Secombe on the telly, and no money left to go out for a beer.'

He's drunk, Teresa realised with a rueful sense of relief as she followed him inside. That's all that's the matter, he's a little bit drunk. She followed him up the stairs and along the landing to the front bedroom.

'Here we are.' He crossed the room to lower the volume of the cassette player. 'Sorry about the mess. Just tip everything off the chair and have a seat.'

Teresa did as he said, removing the pile of clothes from the chair and easing them onto the unmade bed. Velsford sat down at his desk, which was chaotic with files and books. He picked up a can of beer from the floor beside his chair.

'I was just having a drink,' he said. 'Want some?'

Teresa glanced at the bin, where there were already a couple of flattened cans. She wondered if he always worked with a drink in his hand.

'Oh, why not?' She said recklessly. She got up again and came over to him.

'You can have yours in a glass,' he said, pouring it out for her.

As she sipped it gingerly, she looked round his room

138

with open curiosity. There were several big posters up on the walls, one a tourist poster of Goa, showing a white sandy beach under a dark blue sky fringed with palm trees, and others advertising jazz festivals. The rest of the walls were covered in postcards. There was a big brown wardrobe gaping open in an alcove and a small bookcase holding a dozen fat textbooks and some paperbacks.

'Say something!' Velsford said with a nervous grin. 'Don't just look. Tell me it doesn't reveal something too terrible about my personality.'

'Well, I'm a bit surprised by *that*,' Teresa pointed. It was a plaster statuette of the Virgin Mary, eyes raised to heaven, hands joined in prayer.

'I know,' Velsford groaned. 'Even for a Goan Catholic my mum's thirty years behind the times. She think's it'll keep me out of trouble, even if I don't go to Mass.'

'Parents,' said Teresa, taking a swig of beer.

'So how's it going with your dad?' Velsford asked. 'Your mum seemed to think everything was fine when I saw her yesterday.'

'Yeah.' Teresa wandered off around the room, pulling a book from the bookcase, and halting in front of the wardrobe. 'Can I look at your clothes?' she asked, turning round.

'If you want,' Velsford smiled sleepily.

She pulled the door wide open and took a look. There wasn't a lot inside, a jacket or two, and some trousers on coat hangers, then untidy piles of t-shirts, sweaters and jeans.

'Oh, I like the hat,' she said, reaching up to the shelf and pulling it down. She put it on, and looked round for a mirror. 'Does it suit me?'

'Have it, if you want,' Velsford said from his desk.

'Oh, no, I couldn't.' Teresa pulled it off at once. It was one of those black gangster-looking hats; it must have been quite expensive. She put it back, and pulled down one of his scarves instead. 'See if I look like you,' she said, wrapping it round her neck.

Velsford was laughing now. 'Come on, get serious,' he said. 'I was asking you about your dad.'

'Oh, that.' Teresa left the wardrobe and threw herself into her chair.

'It's been pretty horrible,' she said flatly. 'It's difficult to explain. But Mum got talking, and — I just wish things were different, that's all. I wish he was different. I feel like crying for him, but I don't feel angry with Mum any more. It wouldn't have been fair to expect her to carry on with him.'

Velsford said gently, 'I wasted a lot of time dreaming my father had changed, but every time he came home, it was the same.'

Teresa shrugged, but could say nothing. Velsford looked at her closely and went on, 'You know, your mum's done a good job with you two. I can think of kids who've been hurt much worse in families where not such bad things happened. I think that must be because of your mum. I like her. I like her a lot.'

He took a long swallow of beer, and Teresa watched him. She said, 'Helen thinks you're really interested in Mum.'

Velsford waved his hand with the beer can in it. 'I'm interested in all of you,' he said expansively. Then his eyes widened. 'Oh,' he said. 'I see.'

'She's a Catholic,' Teresa said, watching his face. 'She'll always be married, so unless you plan to do something you shouldn't — '

Velsford turned to her, grinning crookedly. 'And haven't you ever done anything you shouldn't, Missy?'

Teresa had to stop and think. 'I don't know. I suppose I cheated in an English test once, but it's hardly the

140

ame thing.'

He waved away her objection. 'No, go on. Tell me.'

'Well, it was just a class test, not a proper exam or nything. But I looked at the answers of the girl sitting ext to me, and she was the one that got into trouble. The eacher thought she'd copied off me.'

'Didn't you own up?' Velsford looked scandalised. Teresa blushed.

'That's terrible,' Velsford said, and threw his empty can n the bin. 'I'm going to have another beer to get over hat.'

'Don't!' Teresa said. She went over to him as he reached ehind the pile of books and laid hold of his arm. 'Don't be illy, Velsford.'

'She touched me!' he murmured faintly. 'Okay, if I'm ot allowed to drink what shall we do instead?'

Teresa looked down at him, feeling warm and reckless vith the beer. 'Let's dance,' she said.

He got her to her feet, taking both her hands and Irawing her across to the middle of the room. Then he eached over to turn up the volume of the cassette player. A voman's voice was singing something slow and sad about ard times and lovers moving on. Velsford had his arms round her shoulders and his eyes were almost shut as he noved slowly round. Teresa looked up into his face and ried to move with him, feeling clumsy and strange, hough dancing was what she did well. When he opened is eyes to look at her, his face was serious.

'Relax,' he said. 'Relax into it, it's okay.'

He drew her in closer and wrapped his arms around her. Tentatively, Teresa laid her face against his neck. They vere moving so closely now she didn't have to think about t. He smelt of soap and lemon grass; his skin was warm gainst hers.

'Hey,' he said, whispering near her ear. 'I wish you were

that little bit older. It's too long for me to wait, you know?'

Teresa felt a tender sadness for him. She reached up to touch his hair, stroking it gently.

'It's okay,' she said, wanting to comfort him. 'It's okay, Velsford.' She was so happy, she wanted him to understand that this was enough, she didn't need anything more. Just dancing was enough; she didn't want it ever to stop.

'Fourteen's too young,' he murmured, almost to himself. 'I shouldn't be doing this.' Suddenly he pulled away.

Teresa, her arms falling empty to her sides, watched him walk to the window and stand looking out.

'Is part of the problem sex?' she asked hesitantly.

'No,' he said, without looking at her. But she knew from the way he said it that it was. She heard herself say, 'I'll have sex with you if you like.'

Her voice sounded so cool and childish it made her wince. As he turned round she saw she had made him angry. 'I will,' she repeated defiantly with a catch of her breath.

'You don't know what you're talking about,' Velsford said. 'You make it sound like a quick walk to the shops.'

Teresa couldn't help smiling at that, which didn't improve his temper.

'It's not funny,' he said with a stiff angry look. 'It's not funny at all.'

'But it's what you want,' Teresa said.

He nodded. 'Yeah, and you'd give it to me, right, just because I want it? Fourteen years old. You carry on like that, and you'll get yourself really hurt.'

Teresa was indignant and distressed. 'You've got me wrong,' she said. 'I haven't, I mean, it's not the sort of thing I go around doing, for God's sake. I know what's right, and I'm not stupid, I know what's safe.' She felt

142

foolish and exposed; she could feel her face going red. 'It's because it's you,' she finished in a low voice.

'That doesn't make it right,' Velsford said, watching her closely.

Teresa shrugged. 'Well, maybe I didn't really mean it,' she said, trying to smile. 'I'd have backed out at the last minute, I expect. Good old Catholic upbringing, convent school and all that.'

'Look — ' Velsford passed his hand over his face and sat down on the window ledge. 'This has all got out of hand because I had a beer too many. I'm sorry, all right?' Teresa could only stare at him.

'Well, even if it's more, there's nothing I can do about it, is there?' he protested angrily. 'Honest to God, when I first met your family, I thought it would just be fun, you know? I thought, Helen's a great kid, and Teresa's just waking up to herself and Nicola makes you glad to be able to do any little thing for her. And I wanted to become part of you all, part of the family. No way did I mean to stir up trouble or rock the boat. But then, I don't know, when I saw you alone that day you were locked out, I started to think of you in a different way, and then I got to thinking about Nicola and I knew I was out of my depth. It was getting too much, it was getting confusing. But once you see a need, it's very hard not to respond, you know?'

He appealed to her with a strange flick of the hand. That, as much as his words, made Teresa feel pushed away to a cold distance.

'You do want to go out with her!' she exclaimed. She turned and blundered towards the door, only wanting to get away.

Velsford caught up with her, grabbing her shoulder and forcing her round to look at him.

'Teresa,' he said urgently, 'don't be stupid. Your mum isn't doing anything wrong. All she needs is a little admiration, a little respect.'

'Well, lucky her, then,' Teresa said, her voice choking with tears. 'She's got what she needs, hasn't she?'

'And you're too young to have what you want,' Velsford said gently. 'Look, if there was no one but you to think of, it'd still be wrong. I'd hurt you and I'd change you, and I couldn't stand that.'

'You're going to hurt me anyway,' Teresa said, wiping her eyes and looking up at him. 'You're going to find someone else.'

'But that's better, isn't it?' he appealed to her. 'Better than — all of this?'

'What, someone like the girl Mum saw you with?' Teresa said sarcastically. 'Someone *nice?*'

Velsford said nothing at all and Teresa realised with a sinking feeling it must be true.

'Louise,' she remembered. 'That's her name, isn't it? Louise the Nice.'

Velsford sighed. 'Look — ' He tried again. 'You only think I'm great because you don't know any better. But I'm not your kind of boy, Tess, honestly I'm not. I drink, I smoke, I fail my exams — I do all the things that you think are stupid. Wait till you get to university, and you'll meet loads of boys, good ones, boys like you.'

'I don't want good ones,' Teresa said forlornly. 'I just want you.'

Velsford face softened, but at that moment there came a noise from downstairs. The front door swung open, and a woman's voice called out, 'Hi, Velsford, are you there?'

'Oh, God.' Velsford moved forward past Teresa to the door of his room. 'I'll ask her to come back later,' he said. 'You can hang on a minute, can't you?'

Before Teresa could say anything, he was out of the room. She heard him call down from the landing, 'Hi, Louise.'

144

Then there were light steps running upstairs, what sounded like a kiss, and Louise's voice much closer, said, 'It's such a lovely evening. Fancy a walk along the beach?'

Teresa didn't wait to hear Velsford's reply. She opened the door and went out to join them.

Velsford gave her a startled sideways glance. 'Oh, Louise, this is Teresa,' he said. 'You know, from the family I told you about.'

Louise smiled. It was a friendly open smile, but Teresa did not smile back. She was thinking how ordinary Louise looked, with her short dark hair, alert face and small sporty figure. Dressed in t-shirt and shorts, she was hardly a *femme fatale*.

'Louise is in the first year at the uni, or was,' Velsford was saying. 'What's your course called again, Lou?'

'Modern Languages and History.' She glanced across at Teresa and added in explanation. 'In my case, German and politics, mostly.'

'Lou wants to be a journalist,' Velsford said.

'When I grow up,' Louise added, smiling at Teresa again.

There was a pause. Velsford cleared his throat. 'About this walk —'

'Oh, yes, would you like to come?' Louise turned to Teresa. 'The sun's just setting, and it'll be really lovely along the beach.'

'I should be getting home,' Teresa said with bleak finality.

'Louise, can you hang on here?' Velsford said rapidly. 'Make yourself at home, I'll just see Teresa to the corner.'

'Yeah, sure.' Louise looked surprised, but she didn't make any awkward suggestions about coming with them. She turned to Teresa. 'See you again, I hope,' she said. 'Velsford's told me a lot about you. You must come up to the university sometime, and have a look round. We could

145

smuggle you into a lecture next term, if you are interested.'

Teresa nodded, but didn't say anything. She was watching the smile there had been on Velsford's face all the time he was listening to Louise. She didn't wait for him, but set off down the stairs on her own. There was half a minute's whispered conversation before she heard him follow.

'Louise is a really nice girl,' he said in an injured voice, as soon as they had left the house.

'I never said she wasn't.'

'Anyway, nothing's happened, so you needn't get yourself into a state.'

Teresa stopped dead and turned to look at him.

'Nothing's happened,' he insisted.

Teresa started to walk on. 'She makes me feel — ' But she couldn't explain it. Louise, in her niceness, was turning everything inside out. 'She invited *me* to come with you,' she said. 'As if I was the one who was the stranger.'

'Well, you are to her,' Velsford said. 'She was just trying to include you. I thought that was really friendly.'

Teresa gave up. He didn't see it. Because he liked Louise, he thought it was all right. And when he's with Louise, she thought, that will become the real part. The university will be the real part and we'll be — just kindness.

They reached the corner. Velsford stopped and felt for her hand, but she moved just out of reach.

'Teresa — ' he said, looking so uncertain that for a moment she felt she had a chance, for a moment she felt hope. Then he said, 'I'd better go. I'll see you tomorrow, all right? At the very least, I'll phone. We've got your mum's party to sort out, remember?'

Teresa nodded. She had forgotten, and now she didn't care.

146

He started to move away. 'I'll phone you!'

Teresa turned, and began to walk very fast towards home.

Her mother and Helen looked very quiet and peaceful as she glanced in at the living room window, her mother reading a book under the lamp, and Helen shuffling cards on the floor nearby. Teresa was glad to go in, glad she wouldn't have to say very much. As she entered the living room, Helen looked up.

'You missed the pizza,' she said in tones of incurious wonder. 'And a brilliant film. It was brilliant, wasn't it, Mum?'

Nicola's look was more searching.

'I'm all right, Mum,' Teresa said tiredly. 'Is there anything left to eat?'

'We did leave you a bit of pizza and garlic bread,' her mother said. 'Do you want me to warm it up for you?'

'No, I'll manage.'

About ten minutes later, Nicola came through to the kitchen after her.

'That was your father on the phone,' she said.

Teresa did not look up from the lettuce she was shredding. 'And?'

'He says he is going to London for a few days, to see his agent and to buy some books. He will give you a ring when he gets back.'

Helen came in behind them and stood in the kitchen doorway. 'So I bet he misses Mum's birthday after all,' she said in triumph.

Chapter Twelve

'There's someone at the door.' Helen danced into the kitchen and stood at Teresa's elbow. 'Wow, that looks good,' she added, poking a finger at the tuna mayonnaise Teresa was spreading on granary bread. 'Can I have a bit to try?'

'Just answer the door, will you?' Teresa said irritably, moving to block Helen's access to the bowl.

'Yah mah capitaine!' Helen tore off again, and Teresa added one more sandwich to the plate before wiping her hands on her apron and moving to where she could see into the living room.

Most of the food was already on the table, quiches and salads and dips that looked good against the crisp white cloth. Across the room on a smaller table were the bottles of wine and juice and the extra glasses Chris and Dave had brought over. Chris and Dave were standing by the sofa, holding beer cans and chatting in a subdued way. They looked slightly uncomfortable in their white shirts and bright ties, alone under the balloons. Teresa thought of going across to talk to them, then changed her mind. Mum would be down in a minute. She and her friend Libby, who had gone up to talk to her while she changed, could cheer up Chris and Dave better than she could.

As she turned back to the last of the sandwiches, Helen came rushing through again.

'It's Caroline with the birthday cake,' she announced breathlessly. 'She's got it in the car, and she wants to know if it's safe to bring it in now, or is Mum around?'

'No, now's brilliant,' Teresa said. For the first time that day, she felt a warm jump of excitement. 'Hang on, I'll come too.' She followed Helen out.

Caroline, Nicola's teacher friend, was leaning against the open door of her car, looking cool and elegant in a long summer dress, white jacket and sunglasses. She called across to Teresa, 'All set to smuggle in the cake?'

Teresa nodded, then turned to Helen. 'You go and stand at the top of the stairs. If Mum tries to come down, say — I don't know, say anything you like, but keep her out of the way.'

'I'll tell her I'm going to be sick,' Helen said. 'Then she'll rush me to the bathroom and she won't see anything for sure.' She ran back into the house to put the plan into action.

Caroline pushed her sunglasses to the top of her head. 'You hold the door open, and I'll fetch out the cake,' she said. 'It's a beauty. I was really impressed.'

'It was a good idea of yours to get one,' Teresa said a little shyly. She didn't know Caroline very well.

'It was a good idea of yours to have this party,' Caroline said in return. 'Just what your mum needs, I should think.'

She leaned into the car and lifted a large pink box off the front passenger seat. 'Now, if you can just put down the catch on the door — that's it — we can go in.' She lowered her voice to a whisper. 'Better not talk in the hall, had we?' In silence they carried the cake into the kitchen and put it down safely on the breadboard.

'Candles, candles,' said Caroline, patting her pockets. 'Oh, here we are.' She gave a small brown paper bag to Teresa.

'I shall leave the decision of when to bring out the cake in your capable hands,' she said. Then, turning to look back into the living room, 'Gosh, it all looks wonderful.

Did you and Nicola do all the food? And who are those shy-looking young men?'

'Sort of neighbours,' Teresa said, and was relieved when Caroline immediately went over to talk to them.'

She returned to her sandwich making and was just scraping the last of the filling onto the last bit of bread when Helen wandered in again.

'Mum's still nattering away to Libby,' she said dolefully. 'And Velsford's taking an awful long time choosing those tapes. I don't see why there's always so much waiting around with parties.'

'Well, we haven't even started yet,' Teresa said. 'And Velsford's taking a long time because he's got a lot of tapes to choose from. He's got to be sure he'll bring the right ones.' She was glad to hear her voice come out so steadily.

'Well, I don't see why Louise was the one who went to help him,' Helen continued, picking up a stray piece of cucumber from the counter and popping it in her mouth. 'I'd have gone. I wasn't doing anything. I don't see why Louise is coming to this party at all. It's got nothing to do with her.'

'She's coming because Velsford asked if she could come,' Teresa said. 'And Mum asked me, and I said it was okay.'

'Nobody asked me,' Helen grumbled.

'Look — ' Teresa picked up the dirty bowl and moved decisively to the sink. 'Why don't you go upstairs and change into something nice? You've spilt something down your t-shirt, and you've been wearing those jeans all week.'

Helen stared. 'Nice? Like what?'

'I don't know,' Teresa said impatiently. 'Why don't you ask Mum?'

Helen sloped off, pausing at the little group near the sofa before charging up the stairs. Teresa heard her yelling, 'Mum, will you tell me what to wear?' She finished washing up, wiped down the worktop and slowly pulled off her apron. Everything was ready now. Velsford's home-made samosas were warming in the oven, and the rest of the food was on the table. Chris had got Caroline a drink and Dave was fiddling with the hi-fi. In a few moments, light boppy music spilled into the room.

Teresa stood in the kitchen doorway, unwilling to join the others. She felt uncomfortable, out of place. Caroline was making the two boys laugh with stories about her school, and Teresa felt she wouldn't add anything by joining them. She looked down at her clothes, long tasselled Indian skirt, floppy blouse, scarf, bracelets, and felt an urge to run back upstairs and change into something else, but she didn't have anything else much, apart from jeans and Sunday best. This was what she usually wore to her friends' parties, the sort of thing most of her friends wore too, but today she wished, too, she hadn't put on so much eye make-up and lipstick. The style was heavy, and went with the clothes, but she guessed it made her look younger, an obvious fourteen-year-old. She was just wondering what Louise would be wearing when a noise in the hall warned her she was about to find out.

Velsford and Louise came into the living room, laughing and calling greetings to the others, and immediately started to unload tapes out of the big plastic carrier bag they had brought them in.

'We've got lots of reggae,' Louise was telling the others. 'Loads of reggae, and then some bluesy stuff for, you know, all that late night dancing.' She looked across at Velsford and her eyes were laughing. Teresa, watching them from the kitchen doorway, felt a pang that went deeper than jealousy.

She moved quickly and instinctively back into the corner where she couldn't be seen, flattening herself against the radiator. She hated her skirt, flopping heavily against her calves, and her bracelets and pendant; she never wanted to wear them again. She felt stupid, raw and young. If she could, she would have sneaked past them all and gone upstairs, scrubbed her face clean and changed into leggings and a big bright shirt like Louise's.

'Teresa! What are you hiding there for?'

The worst had happened. Reluctantly, Teresa turned round to face Velsford standing in the kitchen doorway. He too had dressed up for the party; in his smart shirt and tie he looked almost a stranger, but his voice remained painfully familiar. He said in his friendly, relaxed way, 'You all right?'

'I'm fine,' Teresa said with a quick lying smile.

'You look very good in that outfit. It suits you.' He said it so simply, Teresa was half-comforted.

'Yes, but the make-up's too much, isn't it?' she said, meeting his eyes briefly in appeal.

'A bit,' Velsford admitted. 'It doesn't stop you looking pretty, though.' He reached forward and touched her hair. 'No, hang on,' he said, as Teresa flinched in surprise. 'There's something – oh, I see what it is.' He grinned and showed her. 'Parsley. You have been flinging it around.'

He was standing so close to her, Teresa could almost feel the warm brown skin through his thin shirt. It isn't fair, she thought fiercely. Doesn't he know how unfair it is?

As if picking up her thoughts, Velsford moved away. 'Sorry I couldn't give you more of a hand this afternoon. Those samosas took about twice as long as I expected, and Louise hasn't done much cooking before.'

Teresa only nodded. She couldn't think of anything to say.

'Are you coming to join the others?' he asked more awkwardly. 'Your mum'll be down in a minute, and we should sing "Happy Birthday".'

Teresa cleared her throat. 'Of course I'm coming,' she said, looking past him.

Velsford's smile wavered and went out. He reached a hand towards her, not quite touching her arm. 'Oh, Teresa – it'll be all right,' he said. 'You'll get over it. You will, I promise.'

She nodded, taking a breath and angrily brushing her hand across her eyes. 'I know I will,' she said unwillingly.

Together they went through into the living room. Velsford took her to stand with Louise. He stood in between the two of them, twisting his head round to talk over his shoulder to Chris. Louise looked sympathetically at Teresa and started to say something about her scarf, how nice it was and where did she get it, when Helen came charging down the stairs.

'Mum's coming, Mum's coming,' she announced. 'Everyone better get ready.'

'Where's my glass?' Velsford demanded automatically, raising a laugh.

By the time everyone had their glasses filled and the music was turned down, Nicola was coming down the stairs with Libby. Teresa caught Helen's eye and started singing 'Happy Birthday', with the others coming in a moment or two later. It gladdened Teresa, it almost made up for everything, to see the pleasure in her mother's face, to see how she blushed and turned to Libby in laughing embarrassment as they sang. She was wearing a new dress, short and sleeveless, and the earrings Teresa and Helen had given her that morning. Teresa couldn't remember when she had looked better.

'And Dad isn't here to spoil it.' Helen had wriggled round to Teresa's side and murmured just then in her ear. It was true, they hadn't heard anything from him since his phone call saying he was going to London. Teresa was beginning to think he had gone back to Ireland without telling them.

The singing ended in a burst of cheering and applause and cries of 'Speech, speech!'

Nicola laughed and shook her head emphatically, and Caroline called from the back, 'Come on, it's the summer holidays. Teachers have to rest their voices some time!'

Velsford immediately pushed his way forward and kissed Nicola, then put a wine glass in her hand. 'Can I reserve the first dance?' he asked her, smiling. Almost before she replied, he had turned away and was waving everyone towards the table. 'Eat, let's eat!'

Teresa watched with a painful mixture of resentment and gratitude as he took charge, putting new music on the hi-fi and encouraging everyone to pile up their plates. When he had made sure Nicola had everything she wanted, he went to sit with Caroline and Libby, since they were strangers to him and perhaps needed putting at their ease. From his frequent glances across at Nicola, she seemed to be their topic of conversation.

Teresa waited until last to fill a plate for herself, and while she was at the table a group of three or four girls appeared in the doorway. They were university students, friends of Chris and Dave, who greeted them with welcoming yells, but also, it had been discovered on a previous visit to Velsford's house, ex-students of Nicola's. They thrust cards and bottles at her with giggling cries of 'Happy Birthday!' and stood catching up on school and university gossip for a while. Then they moved across to the table, and Teresa was able to sit down in a corner by herself from where she had a clear view of Velsford.

'All right if we join you?' Only a minute or two later her mother approached with Helen in tow.

'Yeah, sure,' Teresa said a little reluctantly, moving her glass and drawing in her legs to make room for them to sit. She hoped they weren't going to want her to talk. Velsford had drifted back to Louise, and all Teresa wanted to do was watch them. Her mother sat down on one side of her and Helen, cross-legged, on the other. For a while they said nothing, but ate and drank in friendly silence, watching the party around them.

Then their mother said in a bright decided voice, 'I think she's a very nice girl, don't you?'

There was no need to ask who she meant. Teresa managed a nod, but Helen said indignantly, 'I don't think she's nice at all. If she was nice she wouldn't be hanging round him all the time, when she can see other people were there first.'

'Lennie!' Nicola looked round quickly to see if anyone had heard.

'But it's true, Mum,' Helen persisted more quietly. 'He belongs to us, not her.'

Nicola tapped her knee gently. 'Don't be silly,' she said. 'He doesn't belong to us more than to his own family, or to his friends. You have to learn to let people go, Lennie. Then there's a chance they might come back.'

Something in her voice and in her face made Teresa look at her in concern. There seemed to be more involved here than simple good advice. Perhaps Lennie had been right all along. Perhaps Mum had been in love with him too.

From out in the hall behind them came the sound of the doorbell.

'I'll go,' said Teresa, getting quickly to her feet. She was glad of the chance to escape. Another minute and she might have been in tears.

She walked into the hall, hearing the music in the living room being turned up louder. Above it, Velsford's voice called, 'Who's ready to dance? Nicola, up and on your feet!'

She opened the front door. 'Dad,' she said in shock.

He was wearing his grey mac, though the evening was

warm, and his face, above the big cone of flowers he was carrying, was strained and angry.

'I brought your mother something for her birthday,' he said. 'But I see she has a house full of people already.'

'Don't be silly, it's only the neighbours,' Teresa said. She touched his arm. 'Come on in. They'll be glad to meet you. Famous author and all that. And Mum will — ' She stopped, and looked away from his hurt face. She could not, in fact, be sure what Mum would feel if she let him in. The silence between them grew until it seemed something monstrous, unbreakable.

'The thing is,' she cleared her throat and looked him in the eye again. 'The thing is, Dad, you can come in, but you'll have to risk it. There are other people here now. I don't think you'll ever get Mum on her own again, not like it was before.'

He flushed faintly. Then he pushed the flowers into her hands. 'I won't come in,' he said. 'You'll see your mother gets those, won't you?'

'Dad — ' Teresa said in distress, but he was already turning away.

'Come and see me in Dublin, if you want,' he said over his shoulder. Then he walked quickly away down the street.

Teresa watched him until he was out of sight. He didn't turn round once to look back. She felt an impulse to go too, not after her father, but like him, alone; to take her hurt away where no one could touch her any more. She was still standing in the doorway, when she heard footsteps behind her in the hall. Turning round, she saw it was Helen.

'Who are those from?' Helen asked, touching the flowers.

'Tell you later,' Teresa said, closing the front door.

'Velsford was asking where you were,' Helen said,

156

looking at her with a frown. 'He wants you to dance with him. I wouldn't, Teresa, not if I were you.'

For a moment Teresa was drawn again after that isolated figure, moving alone. Then she raised her chin proudly. ''Course I will,' she said. 'You just watch me.'

And together they went back into the music of the noisy room.

Also by Maeve Henry

LISTEN TO THE DARK

Winner of the Smarties Award.

He had run into a little patch of darkness, scarcely discernible from the shadows of the trees, but absolutely different. Even now he felt the chill of it. As he straightened up there was a sound from the same place. It was faint, it hardly reached his ears, but he recognised it. Something was calling his name.

Mark Robson is a loner. Too neat. Too clever. Too keen. He's bullied at school and suffocated at home. But one day he has an experience that gives him a new perspective on life, a change that has implications for everyone around him.

'at times almost unbearably painful, *Listen to the Dark* is saved by its acute observation of daily life in a difficult home, the strength of its central character and the story's positive but realistic conclusion . . . a writer well worth watching out for.'

Tony Bradman, *Daily Telegraph*

A Selected List of Fiction from Mammoth

While every effort is made to keep prices low, it is sometimes necessary to increase prices at short notice. Mandarin Paperbacks reserves the right to show new retail prices on covers which may differ from those previously advertised in the text or elsewhere.

The prices shown below were correct at the time of going to press.

☐	7497 0343 1	**The Stone Menagerie**	Anne Fine	£2.99
☐	7497 1793 9	**Ten Hours to Live**	Pete Johnson	£3.50
☐	7497 0281 8	**The Homeward Bounders**	Diana Wynne Jones	£3.50
☐	7497 1061 6	**A Little Love Song**	Michelle Magorian	£3.99
☐	7497 1482 4	**Writing in Martian**	Andrew Matthews	£2.99
☐	7497 0323 7	**Silver**	Norma Fox Mazer	£3.50
☐	7497 0325 3	**The Girl of his Dreams**	Harry Mazer	£2.99
☐	7497 1699 1	**You Just Don't Listen!**	Sam McBratney	£2.99
☐	7497 1849 8	**Prices**	David McRobbie	£3.50
☐	7497 0558 2	**Frankie's Story**	Catherine Sefton	£2.99
☐	7497 1291 0	**The Spirit House**	William Sleator	£2.99
☐	7497 1777 7	**The Island and the Ring**	Laura C Stevenson	£3.99
☐	7497 1685 1	**The Boy in the Bubble**	Ian Strachan	£3.50
☐	7497 0009 2	**Secret Diary of Adrian Mole**	Sue Townsend	£3.50
☐	7497 1015 2	**Come Lucky April**	Jean Ure	£3.50
☐	7497 1824 2	**Do Over**	Rachel Vail	£3.50
☐	7497 0147 1	**A Walk on the Wild Side**	Robert Westall	£3.50

All these books are available at your bookshop or newsagent, or can be ordered direct from the address below. Just tick the titles you want and fill in the form below.

Cash Sales Department, PO Box 5, Rushden, Northants NN10 6YX.
Fax: 01933 414047 : Phone: 01933 414000.

Please send cheque, payable to 'Reed Book Services Ltd.', or postal order for purchase price quoted and allow the following for postage and packing:

£1.00 for the first book, 50p for the second; **FREE POSTAGE AND PACKING FOR THREE BOOKS OR MORE PER ORDER.**

NAME (Block letters) ....

ADDRESS ....

....

☐ I enclose my remittance for ....

☐ I wish to pay by Access/Visa Card Number ☐☐☐☐☐☐☐☐☐☐☐☐☐☐

Expiry Date ☐☐☐☐

Signature ....

Please quote our reference: MAND